3 FEB 09

Samaraweera, Dar

Vicky had one
eye open /
Darryl

FT Pbk

1863432

Vicky Had
One Eye Open

Darryl Samaraweera

Burninghouse

First published 2008.

A Burning House book.

www.burninghousebooks.com

Burning House is an imprint of
Beautiful Books Limited
36–38 Glasshouse Street
London W1B 5DL

ISBN 9781905636303

9 8 7 6 5 4 3 2 1

A catalogue reference for this book is available
from the British Library.

Front cover design by Studio Dempsey.
Typeset in Bembo by Ellipsis Books Limited, Glasgow
Printed in Great Britain by MacKays of Chatham.

*For my father and mother,
for their support and their stories.*

Chapter One

Vicky slipped into the coma at 2.30 on Sunday afternoon, after having cooked a beautiful 8lb chicken. Her
family sat around her: her eldest son and daughter
whispering like teenagers with the wisdom of old
women, and her husband on the armchair opposite
– *her* chair, a bargain in the Easter sales – watching
his twenty-sixth frame of snooker with glazed and
sated eyes.

In truth, this wasn't the real thing. Not quite yet.
But it did look like it with her head stuck firm to the
cushion she had used to rest on for the last three
months, if any of them looked hard enough. It was a
pose she had chosen as a sign to the others that too
much shouldn't be asked of her, not just now, but maybe
next week. The office would phone in the morning
and she never looked forward to that call, but her lines
were well rehearsed and made any query redundant:
her manager wondering when she might be back at
her desk, a colleague asking how she was improving.
Her family were more used to her illnesses and expected

each new arrival with precise regularity. She was accident-prone, stubborn and weak, and at fifty-nine would only make an effort when she herself was ready.

But Vicky had been regal and proud; slender and elegant like an old Hollywood starlet who practised for years only to hold it together for two short hours, soft lit and crackling in black and white, with skin like a smooth, lightly furred peach. A proper Ingrid in the photo on the piano with enormous smoked eyes, looking bored, without the slightest of smiles. Haughty at seventeen and blown up to look unreal with all the scratches showing.

Now, six inches shorter, with thinning hair and unsteady feet, she seemed to be enjoying the power of her premature old age; ruling the house from her couch, and on warmer days from one of the white plastic chairs in the garden. Very tired and not as alluring, simple as that. So when she made a noise they continued their conversations; one still intent on the screen. When she shifted awkwardly they glanced over, just for a moment.

But she did wake up that evening, with more life in her than usual. She tidied the kitchen and talked to her son, who had stayed for leftovers of cold cuts of meat before he left to meet friends and drink like she used to. The son she had made in her image following in her footsteps. Her younger boy looked just like her husband.

*　　*　　*

In the morning Vicky was lying still on the couch again, contorted slightly after another fretful night's rest; the fat cat sprawled out by her side mirroring the image, more able to snap back to a natural position. Her husband was busy upstairs, tidying their bedroom, sorting and stacking piles of calendars and rubber-banded collections of birthday cards she liked to keep religiously, free to do it now without Vicky hovering, telling him what he could and could not throw out, the former pile small, not warranting the effort. Only when her sisters arrived – both short and soft and caramel warm – did they realise something was wrong. Wrong for them, for Vicky was having a marvellous time. In her head she had started playing like she used to when she was small and precocious: rummaging, unearthing and even breaking. In her head her hair was full and ringleted; a wilful, worldly wise, coffee-coloured Alice, no reflection of the small body being propped up and fed sticky milk rice to give her back some strength.

Pulling on each of her fingers, Vicky's sisters tried to get her to respond to their touch. Stroking back her freshly dyed hair they tried to coax her to keep her eyes open. Her short hair was fine now; straight, silky and black, after the monthly ordeal of clips, a towel to cover the wood veneer of a chair-back, an old tooth-brush, and dye bought from Boots, half saved for next time. But Vicky just shifted irritably, unsure why they wanted her back when she had things to see.

They called an ambulance and Vicky's small body was carried through the living room and out on to the street to a small audience of awaiting neighbours who had filed out to make sure they could be of no assistance. It must be the drink, they thought. And Vicky had threatened this – talking over gate-posts after the shops – had planned an exit, all made silent and slightly awkward now, without the high drama she had always imagined she would want. The movement of her body fired her mind. The hysteria around it just bothered her now.

Vicky's eldest son sat on the edge of his bed with his eyes just open but wide, unable to find a brush to go through his hair. Finally, a comb, one of the cat's maybe, he didn't like to think, realising almost immediately that it couldn't have been. Why would he have packed one of those when he hadn't even moved all his clothes? His mother had told him to get his hair cut as soon as he had come through the door for his weekly Sunday visit. She had said this out of habit, liking the feeling of it in fact when she had pulled him close to kiss him on the cheek, now that her daughter had opted for a shorter more sensible style. Vicky could no longer work her fingers through her luxurious curls, and missed doing that, weaving braids and tying ribbons

4

as if she were playing with an old, familiar doll. No braids or ribbons for her eldest boy, but she had rearranged his parting, pulling back as she did to see if she had been right and a parting to the left would suit him better. He put the comb down and started thinking about what he might wear, what might be clean and ironed already, what would look good with his new pair of jeans still in their white card bag sitting stiff in the corner of the room. Feeling bored already with the thought and the day had just begun. A couple of big ideas came and went, then back again, neither quite managing to encroach on the laziness of a Monday morning with no job to go to; and his mother's thin legs, a little longer on him, weren't ready to support the weight of his body yet either. His head was throbbing. A big night out for a Sunday evening, but still he sat and planned his next adventure, to delve into the delights of the small shops that cradled Spitalfields Market, and the treats on offer for lunch at The Lux bar. He would have to leave soon and make sure to be there on time, to meet up with a pretty blonde ad exec he had met the week before who had asked her boss for an extended break from the office. He would have to make sure he was charming enough to warrant that effort.

Now it was Vicky's turn for adventure. She pushed back the thick, waxy leaves that blocked her path and walked on.

Holding them back as she went, her fingertips traced the contours of miniature half-spheres hiding, yellow spores dotted on the underside of each. Filthy she thought. Not in her garden. But her attention was broken as the sirens started and the ambulance raced the short journey through the busy, suburban streets, littered with empty crisp packets and groups of dishevelled children.

The guilt had started already. How Catholic, the missionaries would be proud. Her sisters and husband in a room together, shocked and resentful – shouldn't someone have called earlier, but who? – and a niece on her phone to Vicky's eldest boy to tell him the news as he couldn't help but think of the nice day that would be wasted in a waiting room. But he hadn't realised yet that her head was filling fast and taking her away, and he'd have better things to worry about even before he got there.

In the last tube carriage on the way to the hospital Vicky's eldest son tried to keep calm, already enjoying the anticipation of the drama too much. The journey was a tedious one, lurching in fits and starts, the train shaking furiously as it passed over the ancient tracks, up and out in the open air now north of Kilburn Park. The train would take him to the very end of the line, the opposite end from where it had got its name. He had just figured that out now: a strange moniker for the tourists to make out and remember, he thought, as he mouthed the word Baker-loo. It must seem quaint when a number could easily have been given to further differentiate the colour coding on the jumbled map. He couldn't manage composure with his teeth chattering and body jarring to an unsteady rhythm so he tried focusing on the group of teenagers opposite for a little distraction, looking away when they looked back too intently; at his stiff back and smart clothes, crumpled a bit but still too carefully planned for this bored audience, at 11.30, going nowhere with a whole day to fill.

Families add to the drama and then offer themselves up in support, and from his cousin's voice he knew his absence would be noted, already had. Poor boy, his mother thought, before she realised she'd have her own demons to battle with here and couldn't be bothered with the nonsense of paranoia right now.

Luckily Vicky's would be fleshy and whole and she was ready and set to take them on. Prepared for the march, with a banner even, if one came to hand; she wasn't about to lose her freedom after years of hobbling. Waiting for her first predator – she knew there would be one hiding – she squared her hips, pushed back her hair and removed the cigarette hanging from her mouth that had appeared moments before.

From round the corner the first one came, and as she made ready to charge she noticed his eyes: full and fearful, scared by what they saw. More a shabby old man than any monster she had encountered in the books she had read or on the screen, Vicky realised she had frightened him enough already and took a casual puff from her cigarette, trying hard to appear less eager to pounce. Even so the look didn't leave his face and he turned away as if he had seen a snake or a spider, moving slowly but purposefully, trying not to be noticed. But Vicky wanted to talk to him, find out who he was and where they were, and started off to catch up, slowing down every three or four paces to take long drags on her pencil-thin Dunhill International, which she finally finished and dropped to the floor to pick up the pace. The old man was hurrying himself now but not moving fast enough, stumbling over the thick roots that had escaped the earth about the base of each large tree, spreading out to cover the ground to find even surer footing and richer soil. Much easier for Vicky's small feet to navigate through, for her to get up close again without any great effort. And as soon as he realised that he stood little chance of getting away he stopped, flopped down on a tree stump and proceeded to take out bread and a flask from the red plastic mesh bag he was carrying in his right hand. Vicky had a bag like that, she thought, except hers was orange and grey. And a little bigger.

There wasn't anywhere for her to sit, the stump a very solitary resting place for an old and weary traveller, and she wasn't about to sit on the ground and ruin her perfectly pretty green dress. She hadn't been interested in prettiness for years, yet for some reason it mattered here and now. This place had a look about it, the look of something grand and special. A bag of sweets had appeared where a full packet of twenty had just been hiding in her pocket. Much more appropriate for a six-year-old really. But Vicky hated sweet things, except avocadoes heaped with brilliant grains of bleached white sugar, so she held out her hand and offered him not one but them all.

Then Vicky realised who this old man might be, and screwing up her face and peering closer she even remembered the small black mole stuck below his bottom lip, looking like something had escaped his mouth the last time he had eaten. Her new boss had one just like it which she had tried to wipe off the first day they met thinking it a flake of ash, not realising for a moment how inappropriate that was, even if it had been. But the old man in front of her was from long ago, much further back than that, it was Maxi-*kolla* – frail and twisted about a weak spine now – whose father had been the family's driver when Vicky's had worked hard to merit the luxury. A very cheap luxury at that, with life-long, loyal service for 25 rupees a day. What a bargain, she thought, thinking of packed commuter trains and buses that pulled away from the curb full, leaving people idling in the rain, dreaming of home. Vicky had grappled Maxi to the ground when he was a small boy and hit his head repeatedly against the hard stone path in her garden – a sprawling space with trees and grass just like this place – for calling her a name. For being too dark perhaps, or was it spoilt? Either way she had got her own back and now, without knowing what to say, how to say she was sorry, she put her hands in her pockets to see what else she could find to offer, realised she had nothing, and so planted a firm kiss on his forehead instead before running off. Alone again, but feeling better.

The ambulance had arrived at the hospital already and Vicky was left by herself on a trolley bed as her son fretted that he was going to be too late. The guilt seeped in and swelled full and sweet – nagging in its insistence, begging for a bite to be taken – as he thought over and over what he had last said to her the night before. But she had longer than that. Silly boy thinking like that – by the time he arrived and was told to sit quietly and be patient, his panic had time to wane. One of Vicky's sisters had left and the other had acquired her husband in exchange to help her through the wait. He had found them all in the corridor waiting outside for information, trying to get her seen. They shifted awkwardly together, feeling in the way, toying with proactivity and pushiness, as Vicky made small movements in her bed just past the doors that led to the ward. As her eldest son held the padded floral bag his aunts had stuffed with all the things they thought she would need (a new nightdress from Debenhams, a toilet bag a friend had got her from the Selfridges sale years before) he felt stupid and paced back to the waiting room to flick through magazines and old local papers, losing his mother's boldness and leaving the old people to ask the questions. But he hadn't seen her at home, not since the night before when she was fine, scrubbing the roasting dish with more force than she should have been able to muster. And a cartoon image from a story his mother had first read to him came to mind, of fussing and crying and people not listening.

She had arrived at 1.30 in the afternoon and it was only 4 o'clock now. How long was there still to go? All the magazines had been read and the food and drinks machines searched out. The old people laughed amongst themselves now, at the other old people, confused, shuffling up and down in search of a working toilet. And Vicky's eldest son kept re-reading the old magazines and imagined being away from there, a concrete block forever full of old men and arguing women with mismatched tracksuits.

He ran out of things to read and went to see his mother. Feeling self-conscious but wanting to look proper he made small attempts at questioning the nurses – no doctor in sight, should he go and have a look? – and smaller ones too at holding her hand. He was surprised by how much she moved about and watched her skinny legs under her gown that kept opening to reveal a ripe, distended stomach. It must be her liver, he thought, the pills couldn't be working. Sitting happier with himself in the knowledge that he might be making some sense of it.

Vicky thrashed about because she didn't feel free to get on and enjoy the new view. Her eyes still opened and closed and she could see things around her, fused together and blurred as her head moved from side to side. All of it spoilt what she wanted to see: the lights, the prodding, the wires that held her in place to machines like anchors around her with hooks deep in her skin. It seemed a little late to monitor her pressure as the pain came on.

In her head Vicky was still walking, the lights above her real body a collection of suns and moons not looking out of place together in one purple sky – reflections of light being just as important as their source. Amongst them she thought she could make out faces and eyes, coal black and sad, but she was too busy to sort the jumble out now; she could see a hill in the distance she felt she needed to climb.

Scrambling over a fallen tree she went on towards it, not bothered for the moment whether she was alone or not, with people watching in the background from the gods, unable to make out the actor or the action clearly. The hill was more a knoll, easy to clamber over with short legs and a long, white, frilled skirt. Was that there before? The ground was covered perfectly with a smooth blanket of newly trimmed grass, each blade pointing straight up, reaching for the sun, raised above the rest of the forest and proud. Only at the top did Vicky realise the immensity of everything around her. Only from this small height could she see bigger hills close by and further off mountains towering above and beyond her – beckoning her and holding the whole world within themselves, with winter at the very top of the highest peak and the dank lushness of a tropical summer hidden in the rotting leaves on the earth's floor.

Where was she going to go next, and who was she going to meet? The possibilities filled her head but the sun was getting too hot and she almost had to close her eyes completely.

They had finally wheeled Vicky out of casualty, across the hall and into a small room to scan her brain. The tunnel should have been bright and white and the motion smooth and motorised, but here the machine was old and tired and the motor juddered as her body was dragged into its centre. The light was pure and clean and penetrated through the layers of bone and flesh, straight into Vicky's soul – the scientists amongst you will probably disagree – and just like the sun, staring straight into it would blind you for sure.

Her husband had waited for hours. Sitting, at a loss for what to do, before deciding finally to return home to his eldest son, who had left a few hours before knowing his mother's stay would be a long one.

Both of them went to bed early, able to shut their eyes and sleep, exhausted. The call came the next morning – not too early, letting them lie in with their eyes open – but didn't give any real news, just details of a move from the outer reaches of North-West London to a beautiful Victorian garden square Vicky's eldest knew he'd prefer to visit. Her husband took the details down on an edge of the front page of an old local directory, looked up the address in the *A-to-Z* and drank coffee slowly and silently with his son whilst they waited eight minutes for the 9.30 watershed and the small bonus of a cheaper ticket.

It was like a day out at first. Vicky's eldest felt proud leading the way, the pleasure of it rising from his belly, which was empty and needed filling. But he didn't expect to see his father's newly acquired weaknesses: the confusion of a new journey, the unsteadiness of old buses, uneven roads and his two size 8 feet. How like a little boy he looked – hair slicked back and tie straight (who'd think to wear a tie?) – and Vicky's son, six inches taller and forty years younger, felt like he should take his hand to make sure he didn't wander off.

From the bus stop on Southampton Row they walked down a small alley lined with old pubs and Italian restaurants. Vicky's eldest eyed the menu boards that stood outside each, marvelling at the value and savouring the idea of eating. The vulgarity of hunger, like all necessities at times like this, made him uneasy but still he thought about lunch and even the possibility of a quick drink later.

They walked in silence through the row and came to the square – Queen Square – with hospitals and mansion blocks flanking the side with sober Victorian grandeur, around the black railings that caged in the large garden. Here the paint didn't peel. It shone white as the morning sun played over its surface; dancing, finding its feet, stretching out its long fingers and warming the cold metal. Coming round the posts they faced the red-brick hospital full-on and walked to the front and in, up stone stairs and anachronistic automatic metal doors. Now they had to search her out and find out what was wrong. Finally time to ask questions and get answers to put their minds at ease, at least get an idea of what they should be thinking, things they had to plan for.

The foyer was painted a cool, breezy blue and the staff were well dressed and polite-looking. The serenity and calm – broken by seeing the usual signifiers of hospitals and death: an oversized painting of the People's Princess wearing a simple black, halter-neck gown; clumsy-looking wheelchairs and sick people – made the place look like an academic institution, the Establishment even.

They passed through, from old to new; the heavy, dark wood panelling and stained glass making way for the clinical white lines of walls, smooth, pale wooden doors and linoleum floors of the annexe – where the real work was done – at the back.

They found the office and the usual confusion, staffed by a chirping, prematurely bald man. People queued intently to find where their parents and children were whilst others booked eye clinic appointments and com-plained about the delay. Seven minutes later – nothing to do but stare at a clock – they were seen and directed up to the first floor where they found her lying, in perfect stillness, propped up by pillows and attached to newer monitors, saline drips and feed bags. The silence scared them, the air of absolute sterility too, that after the last ward should have reassured. With the cleansing antiseptic gel still drying cold on their hands as the air attacked it, the plump, warm nurse explained the procedure that would be carried out. Even the nurses seemed better here: round and motherly or blonde and beautiful, as patients forever expect them to be.

The operation would be simple enough, simple

because another nurse (a nice-looking Australian girl called Maria, his father later told friends who couldn't make it) took its explanation in her stride. A cold metal shunt would be put into her head to drain the fluid that had built up – straw coloured and syrupy, innocent looking, not at all what you'd expect seeing the damage, collecting slowly and putting the pressure on.

Vicky's eldest eyed the monitors as he had the food boards earlier, eager to decipher something from the numbers and lines that darted up and down uniformly, rhythmically; but nothing, nothing at all. The nurse saw his eyes looking and tried to reassure him that all seemed well enough: real problems didn't show up on the screen, the flat line of the final call the only real exception. For once Vicky's blood pressure was normal. They didn't know what that meant. Still they began piecing together an answer when the doctors hadn't started asking the questions. At least for the moment things seemed stable and only Vicky's absolute stillness gave concern; as if she were practising for death, her performance a little too convincing this time.

Vicky's mind had started working hard. Finally no interruptions, no quick movements and, for the time being, no bright lights forcing their way into her head through paper-thin eyelids. With huge leaves for shade Vicky was again happy to march on. March on Christian soldier, march on, armed with a blackened crucifix and a small plastic statue of St. Michael the archangel held tight in each hand. He had crushed the serpent's head under his feet and Vicky was ready to fight the good fight too, sure she'd end up on top.

Her head still hurt a little. Her thick black curls, having soaked up the light, held the heat close to her scalp and made her feel faint. No matter she thought, and tossed her hair about to release it all and cool herself. The statue had disappeared and in its place was a bottle of holy water, small but precious, in the tiniest of the many bottles shaped in the image of the Holy Virgin that the shopkeepers at Lourdes sell to the millions who flock. Always in rows in order of size, in between glow-in-the-dark statues, and sat just under the rubberised contours of bleeding Sacred Hearts. Unscrewing the blue crown she took a swig and felt better already, much better already, and once she had finished it all felt herself again, her head clear and free.

Coming down the other side of the hill, skipping and tripping down and enjoying the gravity, Vicky was at the bottom and hidden again by the trees. If she was hidden what else was? The earth was moist and warm and turned her white socks almost black, so she removed them, folded them carefully but not particularly neatly and threw them aside, ready to get her feet dirty. The mud filled the gaps between her toes

and got under her nails. It squelched as she walked
and cooled her feet as the air hit it. Hippos and elephants
did things like that she thought, and giggled to herself,
surprised to find amusement in the simplest of sensa-
tions.

The forest had become more like a jungle. Perhaps
back on the other side of the hill it was different, but
she wasn't about to go back and check. Anyway she
liked the trees here more and could even see sweetly
ripe mangoes – seamless and perfect with a pale-red
flush – just above her head, dangling precariously and
ready to fall in her lap if she shook at the base just a
little.

She shook and shook, but the mangoes refused to
budge. So, pulling up her skirt and tying the masses
of material into a knot at the front like coconut pickers
do, she scrambled up the tree, remembering just the
way they used to do it, looking like gibbons with their
sinewy bodies and wide, open faces fixed with concentration. It wasn't difficult she found, and after rising
just a short way up the tree's trunk she could reach
out to the tangled branches that fanned out, layer by
layer, rising out to complete the dense silhouette. There
were so many about her she didn't know which to go
for and decided on every one in her sight; reaching
and stretching from side to side, holding on for her
life with one hand as the other teased the fruit off
and onto the soft floor beneath. Looking down she

saw she had managed to displace a huge number – more than she could possibly eat or carry – and so she slowly made her way down, content.

With them all at her feet, Vicky realised just how hungry she was, and dropped down and crossed her legs, untying her skirt to cover her lap in readiness for the mess she wanted to make. The flesh was juicy and smooth, dissolving in her small mouth as her teeth sank in. Savouring and devouring she sat for hours – almost craving, as if she were pregnant again, for more – until all were gone and she was full. It was enough for her here to eat what she wanted and feel full; no one was about to proselytise the benefits of a well-balanced diet. If she had known that at the start she would have saved a few for a pickle.

In the hospital the tubes kept Vicky alive with a less savoury concoction, yellow and glutinous, like baby food, blended and sieved without any lumps, so it could pass smoothly through and in. It held all the goodness she needed, the potassium and vitamin K for her liver and the essence of everything else without any of the taste.

Vicky's husband and eldest looked at the other patients with the kind of neighbourly curiosity that comes from not being able to pay attention to your own home. What were they supposed to do? Looking around at the few beds with the odd relative about each it was obvious to see who had grown accustomed to it all. One mother brushing her daughter's hair, being careful not to disrupt the tube that stuck out from a shaved patch on the side of the girl's head, a miniature crop circle in her straw-coloured hair. Man-made as well but just as unearthly, it made people look harder, the less subtle of them stare.

So they held Vicky's hand and stroked back her hair. Still amateurs, they jumped each time one of the machines bleeped out a small warning. And they knew there was more to come. At least she had stopped moving about and screwing up her face. She looked peaceful; asleep and quiet, so they could take a breath and maybe start thinking about other things.

How long were they expected to be there? Was it a case of holding watch and sustaining a vigil over her body until it raised itself up? Probably. Even if that didn't work they would still do it, she had brought them up to do just that, even her husband, and besides it might look like they didn't care if they didn't.

So the shifts started, but first a break. Vicky's eldest led his father through the square to the station to rest at home for the afternoon. But they took the circuitous route, past the pubs and couldn't help but be pulled in; both good at hiding in the darkness of cigarette-stained alcoves. And the conversations started and didn't seem to end. The old man unfolding all the things he had neatly and discreetly kept to himself:

stories that started before his son was born, stories from years before that too, stories about her dancing on tables. But there wasn't time for it now and he had to leave to catch his train while his son wandered and meandered about, not wanting to go back.

Her rings were removed.

A thick gold wedding ring bent out of shape and held fast, encased between the flesh that had filled out over thirty years, and a slim gold band, dotted with tiny sapphires, one missing, were put together with a copper bracelet and her brown cloth scapular – worn from birth in honour of her Virgin – in a manila windowed envelope. Her husband was at home unable to rest – thank God for the TV, the dish out front and the cricket it beamed in – and her eldest had come back to the ward, joined by the friend he had gone to meet two nights before. He had to sign the papers, a little too young to manage the responsibility and too old for the nurse's warning to take good care of his mother's possessions. But still he enjoyed the thrill, their making him a proper adult in front of her, even if she wasn't looking. Unable to watch for too much longer and not able to talk to her as if she were there and awake yet – he knew he'd get used to it soon – he left with his friend to sit just outside the ward, knowing he was close enough to play his part, jump up if he was needed.

The two young men sat and talked, babbling away and running clumsily into each other's sentences. When they were ten they used to sit like this, talking for hours in the small front room of a sweet-sounding Malay woman who picked them up each afternoon from school and handed them over to their parents when they finished work. She fed them both repeatedly and generously until they had both ballooned into fat, lumbering children. A long shared history, a sure basis, coupled with the warmth of a kitchen constantly in use. He needed to laugh about the past; nostalgia almost offering the comfort of a fleshy, over-ripe bosom. He wanted to be doing something but wasn't sure what. So, Vicky's eldest sat and let this first taste of pain and the expectation of death scare and excite him. And like seeing it in a play it made it easier to manage – the drama exciting the senses but never really threatening sense.

Then the aunts arrived, in time to see the two of them chatting and mimicking Vicky's accent for remembrance sake. Very inappropriate, they thought, not understanding their lack of seriousness, nodding at them both as they went into the ward to find their sister. They had brought one of their own children, who, at thirty-one and no longer a child for most, was still held close and precious; a beautiful girl who would marry well, they hoped. She was the first to come out and sat next to her cousin, blank-faced, rearranging the mottled fake-fur jacket that covered her slight frame, retro fashion that looked too warm for the month. When she was younger she had taken Vicky's eldest and introduced him to her world: early Blondie, streams of eager schoolboys who followed her every movement, and the lines that teenage girls manage to tease them with. She had changed a bit since then, though her face didn't show a sign of it, and having taken her place as a teacher at one of the smarter girls' schools in Putney, she left her cousin to chase all that by himself, not wanting it anymore, if ever she did. The boys still showed their interest but she wasn't playing ball. The years had made her more careful and the applicants were coming in a little more slowly, as one by one her biggest fans found other wives or jobs abroad. Different now, he wasn't sure she was going to help when he needed more distraction. He needed wild stories and silly jokes; tales of good meals, bad dates, big holidays planned for the summer.

By the time the aunts came out the tears were big and full in their eyes and they felt no embarrassment in letting them roll in slow streams down their cheeks, tracing the lines of their face and collecting there to mark them out further. Why wasn't he crying too? But this wasn't a visit for Vicky's eldest, it was the start of the vigil he had planned; and he, more than most, had a hard time concentrating and had already grown tired figuring how long it would be. A chapter a day, but no end in sight.

Would people want to read more than ten?

And then they were off again, leaving Vicky's eldest and his friend by themselves to go back and forth, staying for a few minutes each time by her bedside, shifting their weight from foot to foot, uncomfortable and staring at things that didn't matter. They ran out of things to say quickly enough – all the years distilled down to single images and lines. And they were hungry too, so they left to find refreshments and call for reinforcements. All of Vicky's children should be around her now, for her sake and their own. With the guilt welling up they couldn't miss a minute.

Vicky had been taken in on May Day. Even without the pageants and with the rioters being good, a beautiful English summer – the first of the new Millennium – had begun timidly. With the sun shining, no one would believe it. With people's faces brimming full of summer cheer, hoping to talk it into staying, it felt more a time for birth, not death. How stupid, Vicky's eldest thought: that was spring, what ever really happens in summer?

Walking past the railings again and on to the main road, the two young men started to have their own conversations, Vicky's eldest and his old friend matching each other's pace, neither listening really. The details were sharp, but the points didn't join together to make a whole, sprawling out instead like a foreign tube map.

Faces passed by – some pale and pasty, others olive and full – without connection, just momentary distraction. Then suddenly, all that was human: the scope of histories and futures and a million connections, each one sharing and keeping their own experience. Could they see anything like this on his face, or was he the only one looking?

The faces kept passing, in ebbs and flows, without a pattern, some fast and hurried, the others less focused and slow. The perfect symmetry, made odd with the distortion of hair and make-up, seeming to belie something else – just like seasons, perfectly mapped and sure to come around without any perceptible difference. Yet people still ask: will summer be late? Faces repeated in children, with eyes shining through and showing things they couldn't have seen. Vicky's eldest had his grandfather's face and hands, but he couldn't speak his language or remember what the sand at Mount Lavinia felt like after dinner and a stroll, as the moon shone off the water and reflected the light once again.

The space between the pavement slabs grew wider as they walked, filled with cigarette stubs and dirt; the smooth surfaces pocked, only level in the distance. He looked up and down, from the almost clear blue sky to the filth underfoot, unable to focus anymore and realising that he had tears in his eyes and people were looking.

Chapter Two

Vicky's eldest used to like playing on the swings at the park on Milton Road, scampering up climbing frames afterwards, painted red and peeling. A few years later it was stout old horses a couple of miles away with arching brown necks, all muscle, no bone. His mother loved them too, but for her it was different, the thrill of the chase and money for it. Sitting up there in a perfect position to feel in control, with too much to think about to think about anything else.

The house was cluttered, and a little dirty. His fault, he supposed. He was neater now, and hid his mess in drawers and cupboards and plastic bags stuffed under the stairs. Toys everywhere then. Three children playing in the faces of their friends, never understanding how all that worked, the need to make other seven-year-olds jealous. He swore it was brighter then, the colours changing in his head as he remembered. But everyone says it keeps getting hotter; leaving the family able at least, when the water starts rising, to sit at the very top of Harrow-on-the-Hill, happy to have chosen a suburb so far out.

Then the memory of sitting on the front fence came; legs through the metal-work, entangled, posing for his father and his camera for hours; and the sun hit the ground and children whizzed past on bikes laughing in grainy colour, like one of the old kids' TV programmes they used to repeat in the mornings during the half-term break. Perfect for two hours on the couch with a large sandwich and mug of strong lemon squash that would eventually make him wheeze. Shabby clothes and fuzzy faces with cold, bright, early-autumn skies stretching out through the year. The back-to-school chill that still made him shiver, when things were smaller and London was a little further away – their own town centre the best place to go and buy a smart suit for work.

There was crazing paving in his head too; the image of a cobbled patch in front of the house. His father had put it together painstakingly whilst his mother built her rockery in the back garden, pushing her favourite plants – and some others she had found where she wasn't supposed to, in parks during her lunch break – deep into the cracks between the stone. And both were still there with everyone too lazy to change a thing, chipped and weather-beaten and hardly showing the hard work anymore.

Vicky's children were good and their parents were doing well enough to take them to Florida to see the

sun, sipping Coke and petting dolphins, and then back
to their old homes to see even more. And they brought
back a store each time, holding fast to it for a short
while and then spreading it about amongst neighbours
and friends who went away for long weekends to visit
great aunts who could put them up in Devon. But
they had all liked it that way. It felt good to be on
the top of the heap even if it was small and untidy.
From what he had heard in the playground, the Rainers
at number 14 would surely agree.

Vicky's eldest got fat from all the spoiling, with his
mother never good at getting him to eat his vegetables.
Her younger children took after her husband strangely,
asking for sprouts with their carrots while he focused
on dollops of heavily buttered mash as a sole accom-
paniment to his mountain of roast pork on Sundays.
He hated P.E. on Wednesday afternoons and was a
little too good at French, but none of the other boys
seemed to care too much. A very strange and fortunate
oversight in a rough-and-tumble school. Instead he
loved it all, with the sun seeming brighter and summers
longer, whilst he worked hard and made friends, and
visited aunts who pinched his cheeks and fed him on
demand.

His parents had met in 1974, at a house party in
Bayswater. Neither was particularly young – he was
thirty-six and she thirty-four – but they had travelled
for thirty days on a boat (different ones setting sail

from Colombo six months apart) to start over. And everything felt fresh and new, like a baby with the potential to grow strong, brave and bright, with some hard work and a little luck. But they had left it late and had a lot to get done before those came along. Five years at the most, Vicky had thought even on the night they met; she couldn't be starting all that past forty. Just the tiny collection of photos on the piano to give an idea of fresher faces, the possibility of their dancing and laughing, before they gave it up like a perfect human sacrifice, made solemnly for the coming generation when that story was told.

And they fought.

Things were broken; doors off hinges and glasses smashed. But they held together because a family was everything, so far away from the others they had left, and they quickly got used to talking like that with voices raised. They loved each other too of course.

When Vicky was forty-two she started to lie about her age – even to her husband, who really should have remembered. She was forty for quite a while, and didn't seem to care that if the effort was going to be made at all it was only worth making to be thirty-nine. She kept her hair full; permed and dyed black like her favourite, Elizabeth Taylor, and kept records of it all in a small red notebook, so she could account for each penny and never forget to book ahead to ensure she got her favourite slot on a Saturday afternoon with

Ros. Her daughter had come and she had stopped driving, something she always liked to remind her of. Her smallest, a substitute for her independence – not to induce guilt but to show what she'd give up for a child of hers. Vicky's daughter had never quite understood that one. It wasn't as if she had got so big that she couldn't fit behind the wheel. But Vicky had thought it better to sit in the back, hold onto her round stomach and keep it safe, even without a seatbelt.

Vicky's youngest was a feisty girl for her middle-age, sharing her large, mesmerising eyes that guaranteed she got noticed without having to shout too loudly at all. A match for her eldest boy who liked making more of an effort for the attention; loving it, milking it and playing harder for his audience when the clapping started. He remembered all of them watching him as he performed, dancing and singing and coming out with lines that made the blood rise and faces flush – mimicking the adults with a little innocent cheek and he was on to a winner. And he was told he wouldn't enjoy being naughty.

Vicky's eldest remembered his aunt taking him to see her friends to show him off, make them smile and laugh with the energy of a five-year-old in a new place. And he, perplexed why they had no wallpaper, asked his aunt to give them some money because he thought she had plenty to spare. The thought of it still made her laugh. Her friends redecorated every year, and you'd certainly never see either one of them paint-stained up a ladder themselves. But money wasn't the biggest of issues as Vicky's children grew up; is not when you're five and have a new Lego set each month and even the newest Transformer that only does one thing for the money – certainly not warranting the Visa bill at the end of the month, with it already sat in the corner untouched for weeks.

The children's father had always been bald it seemed, like he had come out like that as a baby and stayed that way. They used to comb the little hair that was left and get it tangled so their mother would have to cut it out and leave him with even less; another toy for them to play with, and all of them for him to look after. Vicky still had her excitement tucked away for when she got bored with legions of friends coming and going, well fed and usually drunk; sisters, nieces and old great-uncles she couldn't quite place. And her husband had Paul and George from the office to sit with in the pub once a month on pay day and an old Pakistani friend his eldest hadn't seen since he was twelve. His two sons were doing very well though, apparently, selling computer parts in their own ware-house just by Staples Corner. One of the boys had just bought a new BMW in fact. Vicky's husband had only just recently shared this news, after listening to his old friend boasting the last time they were in touch on the phone.

But Vicky took her husband with her, to Christmas parties at The Grosvenor House Hotel, The Dorchester and Claridge's, with hip flasks and later whole bottles of whisky stashed between the folds of her silk saris that she kept specially pressed and lined in tissue for occasions like these. Vicky had little sense of money but knew when a double just wasn't worth it, not when you had your own.

Those parties were Vicky's time to get dressed up and show off with her friends. She received two proposals from men at work the week after she accepted her husband's and, liking the attention, she showed what she had that the rest simply couldn't. Not then anyway, not the suburban secretaries and the men who chased them; pale and fleshy and many still living with their own mothers at home. And she danced with the silk over her shoulder moving with her effortlessly, the silver thread sparkling under the chandelier lights.

Sitting in the hospital chapel, much better than a bedside and more what his mother would want, Vicky's eldest kept thinking. Thinking about things that weren't his own, but close enough to mull over and be proud of, remembering old stories Vicky would have seen in colour. Characters linger and get bolder as stories are repeated, talking them into living forever. He wasn't sure how much he was adding himself.

He wanted her back at home and safe, of course,

but couldn't help but think about afterwards – if it actually happened, how to cope – of his life without her, rather than her without her own. The prize of possession. Hold it dear, keep it safe, and be ready for everyone to see you in reference. Mothers as mothers and friends as friends; it was all quite simple. But the thrill of a change, rocking everything and forcing a new look – the same he had heard could happen when babies were born. Maybe it was time for that, he thought, to make a new family quickly. But what a thought when it wasn't all over yet, and he had enough trouble paying his own rent and covering the bills.

Vicky's eldest sat running rosary beads through his fingers, praying for the first time in many years, skipping over words and, feeling insincere, going back. If every word falls into line then that's something. The last time he had done this he was ten and frightened; frightened that the world was going to end and worried why the Virgins kept crying in front of other children entrusted to take back messages to the men in power and the women who prayed for their souls.

A show for the people. Why was the young man crying? Would they look as hard if he wasn't? And the chapel was beautiful and felt right. But it only had a tiny picture of whom he wanted to pray to, mother for mother. So, he twisted from the waist and looked left, away from the altar, his eyes pulled back centre to the light shining through the body on the cross, etched in the glass above the simple marble tabernacle. Giving it life after death for all eternity, as long as the light lasted.

He lit a candle with his fancy metal lighter – cold scuffed gun-metal, buffed to a dull shine, a recent gift from an old friend – almost burning the ends of his fingers with its blowtorch action. He sat alone, liking it that way, as people passed through the corridor outside. And he looked at the piano and wondered if anyone would mind if he played it. Just a little, softly, but he daren't as he was afraid someone would try and stop him, or ask him if he knew one of their favourites.

It was Tuesday already, where had the weekend gone? Not that it mattered; and anyway, it had begun to feel like a job already, getting up early for the train, rotating shirts and trousers so no one would think he had nothing to wear. Uniforms are much easier. Black perhaps? But it was getting hot in the early-summer sun. Maybe a light linen suit? It was difficult to make the decision first thing in the morning when he knew it didn't matter. Anyway, he knew he wasn't planning anything quite so funereal or fashionable for the service. His younger brother would arrive later, clutching a small brown holdall, not knowing how to pack either: a couple of days at the most, with a pair of trousers and two shirts. The train would get him there for early evening, and he said he could stay for as long as needed.

His boss was very understanding, he had said on the phone earlier, and the others in his team could cover for as long as he was needed, checking the pipelines with their hard-hats on, presenting his report if he didn't make it back by Friday.

Where was his father? Vicky's eldest suddenly wondered where he might have wandered off to. With Vicky upstairs, he assumed; the stress of being so close already feeling strange. How long can a father and son sit together saying nothing? He was sure someone was watching and counting the hours.

And that's how it was, taking turns to maintain a presence over her, by her, holding her hand now and talking; even about the episode of *EastEnders* she would miss that night when there was nothing else to say. It wasn't as if they had been able to talk for whole days before, though this time the small talk was filling a silence, not demanding or getting a response.

But Vicky was bleeding from her nose; thick, dark syrupy streams that rolled a little way down, collected and hardened. Was there more to come, held up there and squeezing to get out? And it wouldn't clot, it just thickened on the outside, above her top lip – purple, full and cracking, without the moisture of her tongue.

He found his father quickly enough, sitting at the very back, in a corner, hidden almost by the tall pew, kneeling and praying in silence save for the odd word that escaped and went nowhere. And so they went back with nothing to do except wait for news, repeat conversations and labour over details. The doctors finally appeared, with the reassurance that they had just been missed before but were doing all they could. Such bad timing they had them believe, they should choose their coffee breaks more wisely if they wanted to see them in action. They took Vicky's husband and eldest into a small office, with no room to sit comfortably, but the insistence that they had to before they could begin.

Nurses kept coming and going, to hang up their coats and check the computer in the corner. There was a chart on the wall. It looked like an overview of a school report with names and numbers and comments filling each box. No one was going to be moving up the ranks soon from the look of it. It couldn't actually display that kind of information, Vicky's eldest knew, and kept looking for a better answer in the messy writing, his brow furrowed. The doctor's face was fresh and young, with a look of sincere concentration and calm. Maybe this was just his serious face, reserved for moments like this, able to break into a smile or cheer in the pub after a long shift, dropping at the end of the evening to match blood-shot eyes and a now uncoordinated body. A perfect Pink shirt, held fast around the wrists with expensive cufflinks – perhaps a gift from his wife to celebrate five mostly good years, Vicky's eldest thought – and long thin pianist's fingers with exact, manicured nails; years of scrubbing having worn away any mark. Doctor's hands: cold to the touch and unmistakeably, scrupulously clean.

Finally the seats were arranged, just the two: a large reclining boardroom chair for Vicky's eldest and an old, high, wooden stool for her husband. The doctor leaned back on the end of his low desk, trying to get a little distance. They sat, perched up high, just two feet away. Clearing his throat, he paused, got himself ready and organised his thoughts to make sure they would understand. Relatives could be bad at listening, he had quickly discovered, trying too hard to make sense of words they didn't understand, missing the meaning. He'd keep it simple. But the nurses kept coming in and he had to start his sentence over, and again, never getting anywhere. Finally he locked the door and started his explanation, needing to finish it this time. Without knowing why the bleeding had started, why it wouldn't stop, they daren't do anything yet, even with the bungs of gauze and wool stuffed firmly up each nostril to hold it all in place.

So, another move, another break in the schedule. It certainly would make it easier to look back and fill in the time, thinking how it passed. A week and a half, split in three. Little pockets of time with their own associations: suburban concrete and vending machines, manicured squares and Italian restaurants, and now media offices and sandwich shops. And then back again, with any luck.

They waited for her bed to be wheeled out, Vicky's body swathed in starched Egyptian cotton sheets, a woollen blanket and plastic wrap to keep the heat in. The bed looked huge – Princess and the Pea – and she looked uncomfortable again with a move in another direction. Her stomach made a perfect round bump and dwarfed her spindly legs and hollow chest. Just a hard head poking out like a rag doll with the stuffing ripped out of the body. Even the lump in the middle could be mistaken for some of their gadgetry, the corners rounded by the layers on top to stop them from worrying.

The lifts were vast and could easily fit the bed and the three attending nurses in quite comfortably, but the family, now with Vicky's younger son too, took another one. Slowly, so they wouldn't see her taken away; but they did at the bottom of the stairs, only having had one flight to dawdle over. They walked in silence through the square again, past the University buildings, Bloomsbury and then Fitzrovia. They came to The Middlesex, standing fat and squat, not nearly softened enough by the trees outside, and went in, seeming to know the way without needing to ask directions. They could see her office clearly from the windows by the lifts, made modern with curving concrete lines and glass panels. Her friends were working while she sat, propped up and motionless, and would be visiting soon and asking questions. They'd even have time to get a sandwich before having to get back.

The doctor who greeted them looked even younger than the last, with mousy brown hair he had tried to mould into place with sloppy handfuls of gel at five in the morning – but a few remained unruly. His face was unlined and flushed. Excitement and responsibility mixed perfectly for now, until he had the experience to know better. He looked like he could have been at school with either of Vicky's sons – more likely her eldest, who was sure that this would help. Strike up a bond and ask which college he went to – whether he knew Michael Kindellan at Trinity – and the answers would come to the surface a little more quickly.

The family grew. One of the aunts back again and Vicky's daughter, without her own and away from work, having made arrangements for her little girl at home. The office needed to be bigger to fit them all in, but Vicky's husband was missing so they had to wait until he figured out where the rest had been taken so the talk could begin.

Good news! Just a nose bleed. A bloody big one, but only a small cut in the wall of her left nostril. They must have pushed the tubes in a little too hard, eager to get the help started sooner, and so more gauze and cotton swabs; a simple cure-all. The nurse joked in a sing-song Valleys accent that he had had to use two tampons once with an old black woman, who had flared her nostrils further, indignantly. Did she make it? Vicky looked like she too had come from one of the Caribbean islands – rather than her own tropical teardrop Serendip – her nose swollen and flatter now, her eyes puffy, like the poster on the bus her eldest had seen the other day, the woman in it a victim for being old and black and walking down the wrong street in the middle of a normal afternoon, he supposed. But in the picture her eyes had been open and looked out. The advert worked better that way.

The family craned forward to take it in, getting closer to the young doctor who seemed to shy away from all the attention, leaning back to sink into the comfort of his chair. Two full pints from a small cut – it could happen like that, but they still needed to check and make sure they were right. So, more waiting until someone who could was able to take a proper look with a new toy that could probe away with the help of a small hand-held control – technology all the way from LA.

The waiting room was cramped, only two visitors per patient by the bed, so the rest stood there. Vicky's grown-up children, her husband and another of her sisters dressed in black, still mourning after having lost her only child years ago, and her husband to a twenty-seven-year-old Swedish woman before that. The window looked out on to the back of the hospital, which curled round on itself to prevent too much light from getting in. A mess lay in front of them all: dirty mugs and leftovers from the previous occupants, mostly stale biscuits and fatty Indian snacks. Another Asian family sat opposite them in silence; two old women in saris with oil-slicked hair, sandwiching their respectable grandson, who was taking control. The old women sitting back and letting their boy – the doctor, dentist or solicitor – take over; given the power of a replacement husband and a God-given authority they might believe in.

Vicky's sister and husband talked with proper voices. They had three undergraduate degrees and two masters between them and were proud of the long words they had worked hard to learn. So many of the others were different, they thought. And all the children made fun together, talking in the accents their parents thought they had managed to smooth over.

The nervous humour was rising in them all and would be infectious when it started, spilling over and pulling the others in. They were glad to be here but bored already – they had made it in time and the doctors were busy doing their work. What else was left for them to do?

Vicky's younger son fidgeted around the work surface, rearranging other people's food and playing with the dirty teaspoons. His aunt perched on the edge of the coffee table, breathing heavily in short sharp breaths, trying to fill her lungs and calm her heart after the exertion of climbing up from the Underground. Just like his mother, frail and hearty, her tight black top fitting snugly over her stomach and reaching down to expose a small amount of cleavage. She still had a gentleman friend who took her to the theatre, even if she chose to dress like an Italian widow. At sixty-eight she was the eldest, but she lived like the youngest, in chaos, her house filled with thousands of books and the Rembrandt sketches she had sold her husband's car for. He did leave, after all, and had never once shown an interest in art. It had seemed the perfect way to right a wrong. Seven sisters – four still far away – and all still tussling, fighting and laughing, remembering who had stolen their toys and children away from them.

Professor Anderson had told Vicky's eldest at the start of his first term at college that he did like the drama, and he, as a good student, should learn to appreciate it too. Put the people together and see them bounce off one another. Themes and imagery were for novels and didn't make for good viewing. And still they needed dialogue. It was getting harder to agree. It wouldn't sound right word by word. After all, who would imagine telling jokes and laughing? It would be too difficult to believe on the page.

Vicky's children kept on fidgeting, two pleased to

be away from work but worried by it, with her third and eldest planning all the things he was going to do afterwards. He remembered a job he had spotted in the *Standard* and thought about reworking his CV. Give him ideas and make him work. He was getting used to this already, after such a short time, with something to get up for in the mornings. Such excellent practice for a life of laboured routine.

The afternoon went by interrupted regularly with a steady flow of coffee breaks. No one wanted to eat and instead tried to feed each other like they were doing something important, just as she would have done. Who was going to pay? Another way to delay it all and distract themselves, with the smallest shouting the loudest and pushing to the front with her purse, playing mother to the grown men around her. She had another one in her belly – a brother, she hoped, for her daughter – but Vicky's daughter had only just told her husband, had not even had her first scan. Buying the round of teas and coffees she forgot all about it now with it not quite real in her own mind, at least until she had the chance to tell her mother and see the excitement reflected in her face.

What a proud family, without the luxury of being able to afford it. But it was a lesson the children had picked up from someone – stretch what you can give and it means so much more, they had been taught.

Outside the people passed on their way back to

work. All suited and calm, split down the middle by taxis passing steadily along Mortimer Street. It felt like they had been hard at work too and needed the break, surrounded by offices and people in the middle of the West End, but away from the shops, and for the first time in months Vicky's eldest was up and about with a sense of where to be and when. Eating crisps and sipping diluted coffee they sat in almost silence, except for the odd story – about bad neighbours and people at work. But they showed their interest together, all eager to have something else to talk about. The nurses were good, but the room wasn't as airy as it should have been, the windows too dirty, black in places as each passing taxi left its trace. It was getting harder to believe she was getting the special treatment that all close relations uniquely deserve. But the nurses were good, very true, even better perhaps because they made them all laugh – and as uncomfortable as that made them feel later each evening, it was what they needed during the day. How else could they keep on talking when they knew she'd tell them to stop that nonsense and be quiet, if she were awake?

A long time had passed, enough for Vicky to have rested under a tree, wrapped in the warmth of the ground beneath her, waiting for a little quiet to continue. This wasn't real and the nights weren't cold when the sun went down; in fact she couldn't remember it really getting dark. The sun had set the sky violet and rose again to bring back blue, without ever going away at all. It had been coy, she thought, shy and hiding, but not completely, playing with her until it felt bold enough to come out into the open again.

She was getting bored thinking like this, and the thought of getting up made her feel better, alive. So she sprang up, ready to find something to do to fill her day, not caring that nothing was planned, that she didn't even know where she was going. Every path would lead somewhere after all and she'd find out where she was meant to be heading soon. Time enough to figure it out. Funny that, she thought. When she had an end to each day she let them go by, happy enough knowing one had passed and another would start soon enough. But that wouldn't suffice here with no single sun and moon to divide the days out like markers to help make you feel you've filled a whole life up. She was sure to do more now and get somewhere. This couldn't go on forever.

Just across the road Vicky's colleagues worked at their desks, hers left empty as a reminder. The younger ones listened to the radio whilst the rest talked about how it used to be different working under Mr Watkins. And without realising they were as redundant as Vicky was, as they planned how it would be once the re-structure had happened and they were all scattered to cheaper offices near Morden station.

People started to visit: a group from work and old family friends who hadn't been seen for years. Most went to stand at Vicky's bed for a minute, looked furtively around and left to join the family in the waiting room. Haven't the boys grown? Strange that, considering they'd been the same size for ten years at least. And they patted her eldest on the side and made him pull back; how slim he had got. Another old piece of news to fill in time and silence before they could leave and report back and tell the others how still she was, faking it remarkably well this time.

The phone box was perched on a stand with wheels, sat low on the floor like an old woman's shopping trolley filled with important junk and worthy of the stroll; maybe a small dog sat on top to talk to and pet. The wheels seemed strange on this old piece of technology and with the brakes on, and all the mobile phones switched off, people had to use it with an audience. They were a quiet but attentive one, listening in without meaning to, showing their surprise each time a boss asked when the caller would be back at work. Vicky's daughter waited her turn to call her office and then tried her husband, who needed to pick up their daughter from the childminder's. But no luck, so she would have to go and do it herself, tell her small girl they'd be seeing Granny at the weekend as usual, maybe for a barbecue, if the weather was good.

Without her there the rest knew less what to do. And the sun kept hiding itself behind the next building. It was time to walk and see the real world again; through Charlotte Street, in the shadow of the BT Tower, to see couples eating and drinking and staring at each other without speaking. The first-timers spoke incessantly though, scared of the smallest of silences and not putting themselves forward, worried they might not be creating the right first impression. Keep talking boys and she's bound to be pulled in, impressed with stories of promotions and the new cars and other toys these would allow. Who could possibly refuse such sweet stories of success? But it was too much for Vicky's sons, who didn't want to be reminded just now of what they always worried about, seeing how they usually behaved; and it felt awkward with an aunt and their father in tow. For years keeping the generations apart had felt right, with the memory of the older generation meeting friends from school still fresh in their minds. Memories filled with the retelling of old convoluted stories, embarrassing pictures they insisted on pulling out and the cultural difference that underpinned it and had made them feel self-conscious. How things had changed over the years, giving Vicky's children a touch of colonial exotica now that proved a hit at parties when people weren't laughing loud enough, or just weren't showing enough of an interest in them.

Vicky's eldest looked up as they walked and continued their search. He looked to see whether the
tower's wheel was turning even though he realised it
had stopped years beforehand. His mother had promised to take him to the top for lunch in Benn and
Billy Butlin's restaurant, when the Post Office gave it
its name, as they passed in his first taxi ride, looking
out of the window and up from her lap. He wondered
whether she had ever made it up there herself – maybe
for an office Christmas party before the bomb went
off and the lease ran out – and wondered too if the
food had ever been that good. You paid for the views
of course.

Finding a small empty restaurant around the corner
they seemed to agree to stop the search and Vicky's
eldest boy was back to street level and nodding, disinterested. Vicky's husband looked carefully at the menu
and remembered being taken there years before when
he had met his wife and her friends after work. After
yesterday's food boards her eldest felt sick smelling the
fat in the air as it streamed out of the open door, being
caught by the window panes to steam them up, forming
sticky yellow tears and rolling down. It did do the
good job of hiding the old plastic models showing
what was on offer; rubberised king prawns sitting on
a bed of ossified rice looking the most appealing. It
didn't matter anymore, and hadn't the day before either;
just early-morning greed in preparation for the day

ahead. But this day was almost over and he had eaten enough to see him well into the week already, grazing in the canteen with whoever needed taking for a coffee or Coke, and a slice of cake to go with that?

A man came up the stairs from the basement and ushered them in, angry at having to have made the effort. Too late to make an escape, so they followed him down and found a table. They had plenty to choose from.

Vicky's sister sat solidly at the head of their small square table opposite Vicky's husband, and made the family picture look almost complete, her strong pale arms sitting on top of her round body, looking awkward at such a small table. It had happened like this years before, and was taken far beyond a simple dinner. When Vicky's mother had died during the war, working hard to produce her eighth, she had been quickly replaced by her cousin, who brought up the girls and added her own within the year. She even hid the smallest of them in the chest of drawers in her bedroom when the Japanese dropped bombs and hit the house twice. Not very likely here, they all knew, but the look of it mattered, the picture of a happy grown-up nuclear family about to enjoy the treat of a meal out.

When Vicky was out with her family she sat in silence, annoyed at having been dragged from her home when she could have cooked perfectly well herself. At the weekends she liked to hide away, curl up on the couch and sleep, storing up energy for the week of commuting ahead. She even refused to open the door to anyone who rang the bell unless they shouted through the letterbox to let her know who and what she was in for, and then she would decide. Her husband never understood, she liked to say: he could walk to work in ten minutes. But he did, and coveted the small adventure each morning, the chance of starting up a conversation with a new face.

Vicky's sister could talk. And like all the others she was very good at garnering attention with long, elaborate lines; sweeping her audience along with her, leaving them tired and shaken but usually laughing at the breadth of it all. Though that was never the point. She talked about death – her own sometimes and then other people's – and if it wasn't for the reality of a weak heart they would have stopped listening. Her two degrees came in useful – one in philosophy, the other literature – and gave her the tools to speak and explain it all with confidence, almost certainty. But as she tried to talk Vicky's husband out of his confusion the boys got fidgety, and annoyed because they were talking without Vicky there to argue her corner. And she would have argued if she could have, she would have revelled in it.

The same waiter who had brought them down kept circling, wanting for some reason to have them order quickly and leave. The inset spotlight above his head shone off the oil in his hair and, taking back the menus clumsily, Vicky's eldest noticed his hands: small and clean, almost feminine and composed like the first doctor's. Perhaps he made the food too, with all the fine skill of a Japanese sushi chef?

As they waited for their order to arrive Vicky's sons kept silent and focused on their glasses of beer, almost toppling them over with the attention. It won't be long before the food arrives, they were thinking, is ready to play with on the plate, and eat. And it came quickly, before the boys would feel they should start speaking. Good boys who followed their father on this, biting their tongue, trying to abstain and be good.

The food – a mess of thick white noodles and beef, covered with a slimy film of gravy enriched with MSG and slivers of red chilli – steamed up in their faces. In front of them though it made them hungry and their aunt and father stopped talking and they all tucked in. But Vicky's eldest boy's meat tasted like offal and made him retch. He felt fussy, even though the reaction was involuntary, and he started to remember stories his mother had told him when he was little; about how she and his father had to eat stale bread because it was a waste not to. The story hadn't worked and those times had passed before his memory caught up. He liked to throw away fruit two days after he bought it because it didn't look fresh; wrinkles forming on apple skins with a thumb rubbing over its surface too hard, the other digits holding it firmly in place for the test to begin.

His aunt had fed her children boiled mung beans and re-fried rice after her husband had left and they didn't have anything else. She kept saying Vicky's children hadn't been spoilt, but he was afraid all the same that she would notice, so he moved the food about, trying to hide one bit under another and offered the rest for the others to share as he pretended to be full. The conversation started up again, and without wanting to eat what he had in front of him Vicky's eldest son was forced to take part as his brother ate – focusing and dissecting his meal with the precision of an engineer, separating a forkful and holding it six inches away for inspection, then satisfied, filling his mouth.

Looking for distractions now. The walls were yellow and flocked and Vicky's eldest remembered a story from a class at college. It was about a woman confined to her bed – with postnatal depression or something like that, he assumed, not that it mattered when the story was written – left to stare at yellow wallpaper for years until she began to see something she shouldn't and went mad. But he'd only been looking long enough to remember the details of it vaguely, and they had started talking again, a little louder now, so there wasn't the chance of getting lost in it this time.

The boys needed to get away, but it wasn't that easy.

Someone had to go back with Vicky's husband and sit on the train and talk it over again. But Vicky's eldest always did need to get out for air and made his excuses: should be back on the next train, but maybe not. He wanted to go and see about a flat-share he had heard about in the morning (much cheaper than his place he insisted) and so he might stay with a friend in town instead. It was a large but boxy place near Primrose Hill that he could take a room in through the summer at least. He had been looking forward to walking over the hill, through Belsize Park and on to the Heath like his mother and her friends used to do when they were young. It was all a lot more expensive now. How wonderful and ridiculous to still be thinking about things like this just now. They say moving is as stressful as getting divorced. And what a distraction that would be.

Vicky's eldest left them outside trying not to make eye contact with his brother or father, and walked instead with his aunt back to the hospital. She wanted to go back and hold her sister's hand, anoint her forehead with oil and the soft side of her thumb, and pray for it all to stop or for her be taken swiftly somewhere beautiful, green and safe with a Saviour to make her feel at home and welcome.

He walked on past the hospital, calling his friends to check where they'd be, noticing that it had got dark. The street was quiet now, the commuters on trains or in bars behind glass walls, talking without making a sound, the now drunken banter soundproofed by the double-glazing. Ties were loosened and top buttons undone, and everyone looked alive and strange, like dancers keeping the music to themselves with earphones on. He felt like getting a taxi so he could really look at everyone else, held safe in a shiny black cocoon in even more silence, with tinted glass and speed to make him invisible. But he could do without the conversation: about where he came from (he always wanted to say North London, but that wasn't really very funny, or original) and how the cabbie's Indian friend was looking forward to retirement and going home. He couldn't see one with a light on anyway, and it was pointless going in search when his friends were only five minutes away in a pub on James Street, where Eastern European girls filled bowls of peanuts and brought your drinks to the table if you bought too many to carry. And he knew he'd have to talk about the weather to Tony the landlord and pretend to share in his enthusiasm that all his outside tables would soon be full as the sun came out long and hard enough to make the drinkers comfortable and safe under the shade of his new awning.

But some of his friends were feeling awkward when he arrived, not knowing what to say. It had happened too quickly and none of them had had a chance to share in the story so far, to pay a visit and speak to the family. Years of tales to make them laugh with a mother who seemed the only one to have grown a little wilder with maturity. She could have been a fat lady cooking at an Aga, but she never did like gin.

Vicky's eldest joined the circle where he saw a gap large enough for an empty stool to be pushed in. His friend Edward was silent as usual and sat playing with the ghost of the hair his father had encouraged him to cut off before he got his first job in the City. But he still remained pretty and the girls found his silence charming, filling his mouth with the words that surely raced about in his head. But now it was annoying. Too much for him to comment on – he wouldn't dare – though Vicky's eldest wasn't expecting anything clever or comforting even. It had started to make him feel special, a bit tougher and wise, with more to say. With the taste of experience he could talk about living life and dealing with death at the tenderest of ages. Who would possibly disagree?

They sat and drank their beer and showed their age. Imagine some of them were actually important – or nearly there – saying it anyway to see what the others had to say, and see whether it sounded plausible. And Vicky's eldest was more like himself than usual; pleased to be out and happy too to make them squirm with the details that weren't quite real yet. Making them think he was strong, even though they knew he was just pretending. But he had always liked the idea of being an old-fashioned actor, close up though, without the war paint to hide behind, just the contours of a glass half full and going, the liquid making white teeth yellow and his eyes bulge round. A little dark devil, precocious and needling now, pleased that he could do this when he wanted, finding friends stashed in bars throughout town, ready to talk about whatever he wanted.

Every wall was covered with celebrity faces, framed with scrawled signatures – an American tourist might even think Demi Moore had sat in their seat and chatted to Tony, but in any case would have mistaken her for Andie MacDowell at first, with a face encased in tight dark curls. But Tony had bought a job lot from a friend on Shaftesbury Avenue when he had opened and was now waiting for Vicky's eldest to organise a quick sale to help him redecorate the chipped paint behind them. A drunken offer not forgotten. All the faces staring in and looking sad today. How kind, Vicky's eldest thought; how appropriate, as he bought another drink for them all and flirted with the girl behind the bar and asked for more peanuts.

By the time he got back to them the conversation had moved on and he could take part without feeling he had made them think about something they didn't want to. Edward even spoke. Vicky's son kept eating the peanuts and quickly finished a bowl before another was brought over. They seemed bigger here and although each had a thick film of oil over it it wasn't so bad because they were full and whole like a meal. And he hadn't touched his noodles.

Another day almost over and the pub ready to close. Vicky's eldest needed to look in again on her and feel the chill of walking through empty, leafy squares as if he lived on one and was proud, before getting to the door. He wasn't dressed as usual, his shirt was creased and his hair dishevelled from the wind, framing his face, standing on end and making it look wild. Obviously the man at reception was going to ask where he was going, thinking he didn't look quite right. What are you supposed to wear?

The hospital was empty and silent. He wanted to make the man feel awkward if he did speak to him, but he didn't, and got a nod instead – there would be time enough for uncomfortable conversations another day. He passed reception and up, all the while trying to freshen his breath without anything to help it on the way. He couldn't smell of alcohol, and in a ward scrubbed clean it would carry through the air and stink. But he could see how it might just work, and bending over his mother he whispered in her ear so she could smell him if nothing else – the feint breath of cigarettes and lager making her realise he was there. And he was sure she would get up for a drink.

Chapter Three

Vicky had walked miles by now, but her legs still weren't tired. It was funny how the paths kept on emerging as she went, laying themselves down and stretching on just yards in front of her. And they changed from pale sand to dry earth to cobbled bricks, each coming up from the ground and tessellating perfectly – keyed into place and locked tight, offering the surest of footings. They didn't disappear behind her, and looking back every so often she could see exactly how far she had come and which way too.

She walked with her shadow in front of her, nearly landing on the flat of her head with each step, but just missing. It kept her going as she tried to outwit the sun and make it, not sure for a second why she was bothering. It was like not wanting to step on the cracks in the pavement, but that was for good luck.

She hadn't seen anyone for such a long time. Even the animals seemed to be hiding, and she knew here they'd be able to talk back if she was nice enough to them, interesting enough to elicit conversation. She wanted to have her old dog with her now. The one she used to feed scraps of chicken to by her feet at dinner until her father told them both to leave the table. After he had died – the dog, not her father – the whole thing seemed suddenly unnatural. She had enough people packed into the house to keep her company: a mother and father, six sisters, an army of servants and her cousin Peter who stayed with them one summer and who was the only one eager enough to join Vicky in getting into trouble. The rest were good and shy, all timid little girls, too many for one to be distinguished from another. It made passing the blame easier that way too, thankfully.

Her shoes were scuffed, like small children's shoes are meant to be, but Vicky knew she'd have to get a new pair before she got to where she was going; at least clean them well so she could see the sky above her reflected. It would have been better if they were patent, easy to wipe clean with a leaf or the wrist of a jumper; but the leather was wet and the colour almost clean off from all the knocks and scrapes. What she needed was a place to rest in. A proper home with a roof and smoking chimney, and a large wooden table she could sit at and eat off; with a fire burning and crackling in the background, making noise and dancing red on her skin. It needed to be darker too, so she could savour the warmth and light and play the game of having her own space with a lock on the door and a dog to look up at her and demand feeding and petting. She could even receive guests and cook for them to make them feel welcome. A chat by the fire would be lovely, she thought and went off in search for a place just like that, stepping off the path and moving through the trees.

But the path kept following her, two steps behind, weaving to find space to lay itself down when the trees took up too much room on the forest floor. Vicky wasn't waiting and picked up her feet to cross more ground quickly. Within minutes the sun had gone down for the first time and she could see a cottage, small and white behind the trees, with the fire glowing out of the windows and lighting up the evening outside. She had stopped and the path had caught up, going under her feet and raising her up an inch like the first step on an escalator going up. It went on and found the front gate – painted white to match the fence of course – and stopped just in time before it uprooted its shallow foundations.

She took the few steps up to the gate slowly, opened the latch and heard it swing back and click into place behind her, the perfectly oiled hinges and a snug catch working to hold it firm. The old gate at home needed a kick to open it and the metal had rusted too. It looked like someone was in; after all, who would leave a house empty with the fire burning? And she knew the door would be unlocked, with all the windows tight shut and the chimney too high to offer a way in either. Perfect and quiet, but definitely not still, with the fire reflecting in the glass and writhing on the lawn; and she could smell food too, a whole supper with hundreds of flavours merging delicately together as they cooked.

Walking to the front she found she was right and the door was unlocked, held with another simple catch to keep the cold out. She pushed it open and went into the warmth and found it all exactly as she had imagined: a fire burning to the right with the chimney breast taking up a whole wall almost, two huge arm-chair backs masking some of the heat on top of a dark-red rug worn thin and showing the floor in patches, a heavy blackened stove to her left taking the strain of four cauldron pots, and a large oak table in the middle, ready and set for three. The entire room was open and orange – walls and ceiling – each surface and line absorbing the heat and shining it back. Even the floor was warm, so she took off her wet shoes and paced bare foot in circles, getting used to the space and finding things to pick up and look at more closely.

She made it to the cooker as her circles got bigger and walked around the wall, running her fingers over the surface as if she were blind or in darkness and needed to feel her way. She pushed up a footstool, on which the cat usually slept, she supposed, and got the height to look down on the pots; lifting each lid with both hands and a cloth to cover her fingers so she could peer in. The steam came up and made it difficult to see, condensing on her face in little droplets and running down, so she put them back and went to sit by the fire, knowing she had plenty of time to wait before anything was ready to eat and the guests arrived.

The armchairs could have sat two people on each – two fully grown adults at that – so there was plenty of room for Vicky to curl up and wrap herself in the multi-coloured woollen blanket the last occupant had left hanging on the armrest. Even with the holes in it it kept the heat in and her roasting, held tight in anticipation of hot food with the excitement of seeing the leaves turning orange then brown in the cold air from inside. A colourful and brittle sign of the cold to come, floating down and collecting to cover the ground in a blanket, perfect for kicking up and rolling around in. The seasons would pass quickly if she wanted them to – for effect, as she sat. And while she sat the heat made her eyes half close, and then fully. But it was never going to be dark sitting opposite the flames, with the small spiderwebs of blood vessels lighting red and yellow on the inside of her eyes like fireworks close up. Her mind soon got used to the bursts of colour though, and she began to see other things, things and people.

But the cottage door was opened and shut before she saw too much of that. Two people taking off their coats and talking, certainly unaware that they had a guest. Her eyes had opened when she heard the door shut, but Vicky had almost forgotten where she was and hadn't turned round to see who had come in. And they couldn't have noticed her yet because they kept on talking, the woman lifting the lids of *her* pans and clinking them securely back. A stir too and a taste and the man continued talking to her; caught up in their own conversations they wouldn't notice if she just popped her head round to see, surely? So, she peered and found them already looking straight at her, smiling, a mother cooking and a father laying mats on the table to take the hot pots and save the table. And they were young and fresh-faced, without a house full of children to make them look old. Just her at home now, not one that she remembered, with food and four whole hands to hold her up and hold her safe. So she ran as fast as she could to her father and was thrown in the air after fifty years, her head almost touching the beams in the ceiling. And they all laughed as she squealed – the thrill of being caught as exciting as almost taking flight. But they had to eat and kept telling her she was making a mess, getting up and leaving while she still had a spoonful in her mouth. They didn't even tell her where they were going. But it didn't matter, she thought, they could be back soon;

and anyway she was sure someone else would join her with plenty more to get through.

The door hadn't shut properly behind them and kept banging angrily, the latch never quite managing to close itself. So up Vicky got, still with a spoon in her mouth so she'd have two free hands to push it shut against the wind that had picked up outside. Imagine her being out in a night like this, not at all the kind of thing a six-year-old could cope with. And to think it had been mild, quite warm actually, just the night before.

How tiring it all was for the family. Like sitting and watching the television all day without moving, with all that for your mind to focus on. And painfully boring too, switching the channels just after what you thought you wanted to watch has come on and you change your mind, unable to concentrate. Looking for something else and certainly nothing better than what was on offer. But going out can be worse; sitting in the corner and watching, having to talk when you don't want to, to people you wouldn't choose if you had the choice in the first place. It was easier than that for Vicky's family now, sitting just off centre and watching with a little clarity and morbid lucidity, almost not caring at all. Waiting a few weeks for when it would feel like that completely and saying the wrong thing, and failing miserably, would actually feel quite good.

Heaped on high, ready to break and enjoying every second. Much better than looking for truth at the bottom of a grubby pint glass or wandering down Kilburn High Road assessing the damage as the sun comes up and the rest are happily tucked up with people whose names have slipped their mind. But they can find it all out again when they go for coffee with friends and laugh about pouncing and falling over and not caring for a second what they must have looked liked. That was it. Always caring too much you forget the rules and aren't allowed to play. At least Vicky's boys usually left with the creases still in their trousers and mint-fresh breath someone would love to feel over their face and down the back of their neck.

Wallowing like pigs. Vicky had a better time of it with the mud for sure.

Vicky's eldest had been thinking back to a party in West Hampstead and the walk home through Kilburn. Not very considerate for the reader, or the writer for that matter, making the whole job a lot more difficult. That was how it worked, with things coming back to him as he sat with the perspective skewed: faces that looked like someone he had seen before, or the flat body of the Middlesex and stuck-on luminescence of its moon-faced clock sat just above the mouth of a curved attic window displaying a white dressing screen and a thin, hunched human silhouette for people to see. Two small windows like nostrils made the face complete, looking like a train face from *Thomas the Tank Engine*, blown up and held high, sitting still and sad-looking, but still reminding him of that long-lost toy. All this just over his shoulder as he passed on his way to Tottenham Court Road tube late on Wednesday night – most of the pubs he liked seemed to be somewhere around there anyway, so he would be retracing these steps for some time to come.

And Vicky's story had begun to get interesting. But it had been a while since her eldest had seen her eyelids flicker.

Vicky's eldest's bed was too hot. He was back at his parents' home in his old room, having not been invited to crash with a friend the night before and worried his own place would feel too comfortable away from the family and silent waiting. The place was familiar enough, it had been home for years up to just a few months ago, and was still home to him when he wasn't too tired to make his way back on buses or trains or both for free meals and some money. The room still had most of his things in little messes on the floor – even the cat, up two flights to find another body to sleep next to and on. He hadn't even bothered to take his books to his new place yet, though he knew that was a good thing now, he'd be here for a while at least. And it was better like that anyway, for show, so guests could ooh and ah at his first flat all his own, looking good without the clutter, a cleaner carpet and higher ceilings.

His bed rattled every time a train passed, one of the cons of living so close to the station. Amazing how he had learnt to sleep through it, though at 7 he awoke, alert even with his head heavy. Maybe it was the memory of getting up for school, the memory of waking up without an alarm and with a clear head, the energy to see the day through. It was useless now anyway, they would all wait for the rush to subside however early they raised themselves from their beds. And there'd be three of them for the bathroom, with his younger brother back in his old room too, all needing to be ready at the same time, so he might lie in and wait for his brother and father to leave and follow them on the next train.

The antediluvian timetable wasn't the most reliable – having seen much more than a mere flood – and yet Vicky's eldest checked it without taking in the numbers; clearly an old habit he hadn't shaken. It was only a fifteen-minute journey in any case, once the train came and got going again, having picked up people from fifty miles away taking less routine journeys.

Vicky's eldest had always liked travelling by himself. He looked out of the window most times, more at his reflection than at the things that whizzed by, never able to bring himself to read a book, the journey too short to get very far. Perhaps a paper but never a book, and nothing at all if he had to stand. But if there were seats – lots of them, so he didn't have to work hard avoiding other people's eyes – he could sit and look out of the window and enjoy what passed him at speed. A good time for all the same ideas to unfurl in his head, repeated daydreams of future achievements playing like perfect film scenes to occupy him, with each of the rides identical themselves. He certainly wasn't going to be able to tell any of them apart. Like Sunday mornings in after Saturday nights out: the papers, some TV and a roast.

The train stopped just outside Willesden Junction; the huge yellow crane on his right as stationary as ever with a sign reading: 'National Railways of England, Scotland and Wales'. That high up they weren't going to change the wording each time its owner was re-christened. It reminded him of *Star Wars*, he thought. Like a clumsy mechanical camel, an AT-AT with four thick legs held square and poised, ready to move off if a rider made it all the way up to pull their leg back and kick off at a canter. Heading east to Gospel Oak. He wondered if you could get it to turn round the other way without it falling over. Much better to trot to Ledbury Road, careful not to run flat into the side of Trellick Tower first, to have a look at the clothes, some books and the pubs.

If he looked closely enough he would have seen that the tracks were already being warped and buckled by the heat – it having only just come on strong for the summer – and the driver waited patiently for a sign to go when no one else seemed to be in the way. And then the engine started up again with an apology first in the manner of a flight attendant, echoed at Euston five minutes later as all the passengers were asked to remember their belongings and have a nice day. How long a part of the training had that been?

It made it seem like a longer journey, one that required baggage with tags and refreshments along the way, maybe a smoking carriage too. And the day-out feeling had started again. He did quite feel like going to the cinema and picked up a paper to see what was on. It was strange how he had got good at organising his time, packing it all in with visits and dates as breaks, with everyone else following his schedule perfectly. He had to sort out his flat too, get second opinions from friends whether it would be a good idea to tell his landlord he was leaving and move back home. Without the advice it rested on his head, like a jug of water that needed carrying a very long way very smoothly, with people looking, waiting for you to spill some, with the rent and bills piling up and no money to pay for them. It had been a stupid idea in the first place – the feeling he was too old to be at home –

particularly when he had only just popped in for five minutes to take a quick peek at lunch as the people in the office he was temping in hadn't invited him to join in their midday plans. And it had been small – built for a student, a very professional MBA though – forcing the current occupier to spend too long in the airier confines of his desk at the library. But it was tucked in the roof space with all the beams exposed, and the whitewashed walls shone with the light that flooded in through skylights above. A glass-top table would look good in the corner, and in his head the room grew two feet and could easily accommodate a big chair so he could sit and look out of the window to a pretty pastel terrace opposite. Just until he got a proper job, met someone nice, and could start searching for a bigger place across the street behind one of those powder-pink or blue facades.

Vicky's eldest met the others back in the waiting room and craned his neck to see his sister arrive. It was just like waiting for her at the end of each term after ten weeks with the other boarders, under strict supervision together until their release. The result of a little rebellion at thirteen; she had been lucky not to have been sent back to Sri Lanka to live with an old aunt who would have been stricter still. Each holiday she would return with the faint trace of make-up still on her face and freshened-up smoke on her breath, Vicky's sons waiting for her expectantly like a treat. Much more fun than a puppy at Christmas and good company for the boys through the summer with weeks of stories to share as they sipped chocolate milkshakes from McDonald's each afternoon and watched the TV, young enough still to enjoy simple pleasures like that.

It wasn't the most exciting way of whiling away the summer, not the kind any of them would repeat to friends to get them jealous in September; but with each of the three so close in age it felt like camp, with no one playing the babysitter and exerting false authority. The school wasn't doing the trick and Vicky's daughter was having too much fun, already meeting boys and smoking, wearing what she wanted on Saturday nights even if it meant sneaking out through windows after dark and changing in a pub toilet. But that had been years ago and she was married now with another baby on the way, more settled than either of her brothers, her new family picture complete. They had their own place, one she had made her own, stripping old wallpaper, plumbing in the bathroom sink and carrying a chest of drawers in pieces from Ikea with her first bump growing – building her nest with flat-pack furniture and a large tin for a clean lick of paint; doing the hard work like a tribal mother as her husband made the money to buy the other things they might need. Trekking through a wasteland on her way home from furniture shops and balancing pots of matt and gloss as she went, with increasingly unsteady feet underneath refusing to give way.

But Vicky's daughter had a new leafier patch in North-West London now which didn't really resemble any proper wasteland. Thankfully it had been a warm Easter the year they moved so the greyness of the concrete flyover nearby cheered itself up with the extra light, ready for their arrival, and the blossom on the trees was given the chance to come to the foreground. After school and just eighteen there had been a year of living above a shop on her own on Essex Road and, before, a short stay in a student house in Bethnal Green. She had moved quickly after she had seen a man pushed up against her window; the flesh of his back sinking into the spaces between the bars that protected the pane, a hand hitting his head hard onto one of them. Calling the police and waiting so long she went out herself, hollering until they both left, the man with the cracked head a little more slowly than his friend.

Vicky's daughter was the only one with a Singhalese name, the little princess, contracting it for simplicity, fed up with having to spell it out for the form fillers and over the phone at work, even to her boyfriend at first who hadn't known where to find the little island on the map. She got her first job wearing a uniform as she moved west to move in with him, standing short behind the front desk and dealing with drunk men who shouted abuse and once even lifted her clean off her feet to pull her face to face with them over the high top. The women were worse, she said, from the same estate she lived on with her boyfriend, his mother, three sisters and their collection of small children, all different shades of brown, with hair ranging from fine and auburn to thick, tight chocolate-brown curls. Vicky's daughter was called *coolie-girl* by the men who whistled at her on Ladbroke Grove, having turned nineteen with her own hair permed to mimic a Goldilocks afro, mixing her Asian roots with a bit of black body, kissing her teeth to fit in and hold her own as old Jamaicans and young Pakistanis speaking in surprisingly similar voices jostled by. Her voice had come full circle now, and even her boyfriend had managed to smooth his over after they married and had a daughter who might start copying the intonation.

Everyone wore gold on the estate, chunky and shiny, dripping from fingers and ears and weighing down people from the neck. She had bought Vicky's eldest son his first ring, heavy and square, which stood proud of his long, thin fingers. Christmas 1995, just five years ago, but seeming like another time, the first year she had money to buy proper presents with three pay cheques having passed swiftly through her bank account, torn to pieces and distributed liberally along Oxford Street and the old jewellers and pawnbrokers in Notting Hill.

Living right in the heart of it, just two streets away from where the media men and girls with trusts were investing in finer London stock, but not a long bus ride from the shops she still went to (now driving a Golf with a child-seat), skirting along the top edge of the park, through Bayswater and Notting Hill to Westbourne Park and Ladbroke Grove. Seeing the gaudy paintings lining the railings on weekend afternoons, laden down with plastic shopping bags, the more the better, to show she was an adult and had things to spend all her new money on – certainly no respect given to those who saved, under mattresses and at the post office. Huge families living together in rough stone cubes scattered amongst buildings all facing in on each other. The children used the narrow gangways outside each stretch of doors as their playground – Billy at number 73 had sprayed his territory like a cat and hated it when the neighbours came and went from their flats and disturbed the clear path just perfect for his bike – dropping things from great heights, on people's heads, trying to go about their day, who had to move swiftly through and up via the stairs with the lifts not working.

The teenagers sat in cars to one side, second-hand 4x4s with miniature steering wheels, padded with dimpled racing leather, and shiny alloy wheels. All four doors open and music shaking the whole body, with four seats, heads in, legs out and trails of smoke –

whatever they could get their hands on: weed from a big brother or singles from Mr Singhe at 10p. One girl to every three boys, with their hair perfectly parted and slicked flat with gel and water to the contours of their head, pulled tight up to give a premature face lift, and then falling in hard corkscrews and waves from up high to cover ears and neck in flecks of brown and brittle copper blonde.

Everyone chewed gum and talked whilst moving it about to each corner of their mouths. Like experts: saxophonists trained not to need to take a breath whilst emptying their lungs. But Vicky's daughter was a little too old to do that, and could always make out her boyfriend's eldest nieces at fourteen teasing young men her own age, stamping feet up and down to keep the warmth in, the heat of the smoke circulating inside their slight girlish bodies.

She had done this all before at school, but as always it seemed, looking back, more innocent: posters of Ralph Machio (the Karate Kid), Michael J. Fox and Duran Duran pulled from the centre pages of *Smash Hits* and replaced as her tastes changed and she hit her teens and pictures of newer talent filled the press. She still had the cap her father had bought her from a pier in Blackpool when she was ten, the face of Simon Le Bon emblazed on the top to be spotted by the taller children and adults who looked down. She had no reason to keep that, but had, at the back of a drawer, along with diaries and letters and a couple of silly souvenirs from other family outings.

Blackpool – just before the clubs full of stags and hens really got going and the majority of people walking down each pier were well into their sixties, or under ten and on bikes. It made it easier, with Vicky's children less conscious of looking different; even though the old people noticed more they were less likely to say anything loudly in the streets. And away from London people did sometimes say things, less used to integrated variation. Talking over their parents' accents and trying to hide the signs that made them sound and look like another Indian family, especially when their parents were from Sri Lanka and couldn't really manage even that language. Writing it was even worse, with the letters curling round on themselves like a long line of miniature snail shells requiring a good, skilled hand – if the end of a sentence was ever reached. Vicky's husband had had a hard time teaching physics in Singhalese before he came – the old language newly reinstated by Mrs Bandaranaike in honour of her long-assassinated husband – especially as he could just about order fresh fish off a cart from the man at the end of the street.

And so the opportunity for a new life in his thirties, sitting in pubs where his children would sit twenty-five years later, letting the excitement flow through his right arm, down to his pen and onto the almost transparent blue paper that had to be held down with the straight of his left as he wrote with his right so it wouldn't blow away when the door was opened. A shaky hand and his mother might think the ice had got into his bones as she feared it might. It just wasn't right to go all that way and freeze, with a toffee-coloured body meant to be warmed and then leathered by the sun over the years. In each letter he put money, a quarter of his wages in crisp notes wrapped in black sheets of carbon paper to keep them safe, away from prying eyes. It was like the old woman was being paid in arrears too, the first one taking well over six weeks to get to her.

Vicky's husband had had an aunt to stay with when he arrived but that didn't last long, and having already spent the first night on a bench in Hyde Park because he didn't quite know how to get to Walthamstow — even know if that was how you pronounced the word — the offer of support had at least kept a family back home happy. He found his own room soon enough, with others just like him; some he knew already and others he didn't; until, polishing off a whole bottle of whisky and old, vague connections, right and wrong, were dug up and asserted. Raj, with whom he shared a room, wasn't even Singhalese, but it didn't matter because if Vicky's husband shut his good eye and half closed the other he looked just like Uncle Aloysius. He was the one who became a priest and then took a mistress at forty-eight, though he never left the priesthood. It was a calling and this was a singular weakness. It wasn't as if he drank or gambled for money.

The building Vicky's husband found on Queensborough Terrace housed another distant cousin in the basement and that cousin's parents in the loft. It was called the Apollo Hotel, and still was, he had just found out, and was the product of two old stucco-fronted houses being knocked together, with all the original features ripped out and not even sold at auction. It made cleaning easier, and it was more secure with sheets of safety glass replacing the old ornate lead-lighting above the two doors and circles of brittle air with numbers painted on: 96 and 98. Each one of the inhabitants passed through the streets singing to themselves, humming softly instead, if someone looked their way. The new life had started even if there wasn't enough work and the room was damp and dark and they missed having real friends. And they felt like teenagers again, without the politics and pessimism of too much experience. At least nothing that would help them understand their neighbours and new colleagues. That would come later and they'd be wrong of course, seeing the divisions twenty years after they had come when face-to-face it passed them in the streets now. As they kept on singing: songs from Country greats, songs that were about the simplicity and naturalness of finding a wife and having children; songs that made them seem innocent and green when the music had changed so much and the people around them were all moving to a new rhythm. They couldn't imagine that thirty years later people their age would waste time worrying that it wouldn't happen to them: men and women writing about the cult of singledom; the torture, the pain, the affliction of being thirty and not knowing who would go the distance with you. But Vicky's future husband and the men he lived with were different, sitting in pubs and pushing themselves forward – innocently approaching women on the streets, on the bus and at any of the parties which usually were just gatherings round a table in one of their rooms with a bottle of cheap whisky when the beer money had run out.

Just one year later and two of them had managed it, the products of assured minds. Vicky searched out and married, with Raj finding Helen, an eighteen-year-old girl fresh from North Wales and ready to dabble in everything London, even by way of Kerala. She sang in bars at night and cleaned offices in the day and shopped on Portobello Road with Vicky for the cheapest baby-grows in readiness for the children they were carrying. Instant families for two men away from home, and neither had even thought of going back for a moment. It would have taken too long anyway and the voices had grown faint without the luxury of a telephone.

Walking along Bayswater Road only a little further west from where Vicky's eldest son found himself every other Friday, visiting his friend Ruth for *Shabbat* supper in a beautiful townhouse with all the trimmings in place. A world apart, with a Hungarian maid serving the potatoes with a smile.

Everything had come together on this small square of the map: the northern shoulder of the park and a little further beyond. But the family hadn't been there together for years, not since Helen had moved back to Wales with her ten-year-old son, several years after finding out about Raj's serial affairs. Always with European women – almost like he wanted a Western woman but needed *some* colour in their cheeks. A string of Marias, Carolinas and Lauras, the middle vowels stretching beautifully to make the last Italianate, arching like the base of her neck and long back, the sound itself a little too fitting for that move. What an adventurous one he was.

Sitting on top of the tall cabinet in the front room at home was a collection of old photos and pictures so high up that no one could actually see them. A black and white shot of Vicky's parents carrying a small fat baby, probably one of the cousins; a shot from one of Vicky's office parties, and a pastel almost entirely in blue and brown of Vicky's younger son.

It was first Holy Communion day for Vicky's

younger boy and he looked serious and sweet in a pale-blue shirt and wide navy tie. Black trousers like the rest and hair so neat it would be impossible for any of the newly graduated art students in Hyde Park to make it look real – a perfect rendering of a human face and the too shiny hair that could have been lifted from a doll's head. The sun came into the background, and a nondescript light sky was drawn, one that could have been a backdrop but should have been trees and moving people, the stationary ones craning over the artist's shoulder and easel to see if he was getting it right and if it would be worth the time and money to be next. June 3, 1984 and the family were tucked away in their small house in a faraway suburb, with the added bonus of a disused toilet outside they could use as a shed, a newly fitted bathroom inside and a wide garden for the three children to play in. But they were pulled back in for the day to walk over a larger lawn with swans and duck and groups of people paddling in boats on the Serpentine. A special day: a treat after the service, whilst they were adventurous enough for the whole of London to be just a number of stops away on the tube. No one would imagine it as the years went by and the routes became set; to work and back, socialising closer to home. Helen and Raj were still in their flat then, close by on the Hallfield Estate, filled with toys for the children she looked after as her husband slept in the big bedroom (only called that in relation to the other). He slept through the day in readiness for his nightshift so couldn't join his wife to watch the picture of Vicky's little boy being drawn. He was in truth preparing to chase a few new pretty faces and drink from large bottles of duty-free spirits, smuggled in battered cases by old aunts and newer friends visiting. He had hidden them carefully behind his shoes, under the bed, to take with him later for the long night ahead.

Darting about on one long road: two miles and twenty-five years. Vicky had stopped still for the moment but had already covered a lot more ground than that. Such a familiar road for them all, running from Marble Arch into West London like a fat artery with tiny branches reaching north and the green chest of a park to support it underneath; easily spotted on night bus maps when your eyes are playing tricks and everything's flipped upside down and whirling still.

Chapter Four

In all the stories you read about epic journeys one thing is clear: the man on the march is walking to save his soul, battling evil in the guise of men with swords and soft-breasted women swimming together in hidden lakes, calling him to join them and break his journey. But Vicky knew all of this already and wasn't about to get distracted, even though she was ready to enjoy what she found on the way for a short while. She wasn't stupid, and if she felt hungry she knew she'd have to stop for a bit. Marching on her stomach like every good soldier. It meant she'd be able to go a little further.

Vicky was still eating in the cottage when the sun came up. It worried her to think how much she had managed to get through, her small belly full, round and hard, a tight drum she could pat. Checking the four pots she saw that they were still brimming full – she hadn't even scratched the surface, her spoon lost in the cavernous filled hollows. Each seemed to have cooled and a skin had formed to protect what lay beneath and playing with one she broke the seal again and delved in to find the contents still piping hot. Perfect for a cold winter's night, but it was light now, and judging by the fierce triangles of light and heat shining in through the windows she could tell it was warm too and yet the food kept giving off heat inappropriately. She closed all four lids, sure they would keep if she needed another feeding, and hopped off her chair to find her shoes, clean them a little and put them on. But what was she going to clean them with? A bit of spit and polish would have to do, and with a little hard labour and the help of one of the cloths on the table she had them looking perfectly new – the magic of the place making this small miracle possible.

She shut the door behind her, leaving the fire burning. It would go on forever she knew, never having replaced any of the wood herself; meaning, of course, it would have been impossible to get under control and put out even if she had wanted. She felt better leaving it all as she had found it. Her eldest boy had just learnt how to build one from scratch in an old farm house in North Yorkshire, using twisted-up news-paper to create a pyramid, setting that alight and slowly adding lightweight kindling so it caught and only then the wood, small pieces first before the heavy logs. Nurturing it so it could warm you, whilst looking out to the moors you had to imagine were all around you, hiding in the darkness. Vicky hadn't a clue about any of this and if she was going to come back she wanted to make sure the fire was ready and waiting for her. What was the point of shelter without one?

It was warm outside, quite hot in fact, and her light dress was more than sufficient, if not a little too much for the weather if a breeze didn't pick up. She pulled up the frilled sleeves, puckered around her thin biceps, as far as they would go and started marching forward, down the path, through the gate and right at the flat stones that met it. But the path wasn't going anywhere, and without wanting to let her concern show she kept going, looking over her shoulder and waiting for it to catch up and show her the best way. After all, it had led her here when she needed a roof and food and fire, even if she had outwitted it for a few short seconds she couldn't deny it had pointed her in the right direction, holding back only at the end to make her feel like a grown-up.

But it still was set firmly in the ground and Vicky wasn't ready to turn back because of a path's stubborn insistence. She was the stubborn one, the headstrong one, the one who was moved through four schools in Colombo before finally finishing, because they didn't quite get how she did it: pyromania in the science labs and some creative interpretation when she had to read for the class. So she'd find adventure herself, with lots more to rummage through before she found her way. No problem at all. She was looking forward to it.

★   ★   ★

Away from her the days were long, difficult to even imagine each winter, stretching from the very early hours to nearly nine. The more the sun shone the more they could do, like farmers. And after a long day by a bedside the evening could begin like a morning and have a chance to take flight before it got dark. There was even time to do other things, look in shops and catch a film, but there wasn't anything good on. So it was a small number of close-by pubs instead, and hours in front of the TV. Watching repeats of *Seinfeld* and *Frasier* each night coming in through a new cable, digitally compressed and thrown through the air to the small disc stuck above the house's front door. Vicky's children did like the American ones and could sit now and watch whole series as they waited.

Vicky's eldest never made it to closing time. That wouldn't do. Too much drink and with the long journey home there'd be no chance of getting in before midnight. So 10 was the watershed, a turn of a key that refused to turn at first, and the unsurprising discovery of his father and younger brother sitting in the corner – Vicky's husband on her chair again, and her younger son on the sunken cushion where a spring had given up its fight at the end of the couch that usually supported her feet. And the repeats repeated themselves: two clever brothers (a few years on, of course) and their older father, with white hair and a stick, the difference between the generations scripted and spoken perfectly and good for a laugh, but usually not out loud. More a case of knowing nods, understanding the jokes and having a feel for the characters. The bad accents coming from some of the supporting cast didn't even matter.

Another move that night, back through the same streets they had used before like a memory playing in reverse with the lights off and everything they had noticed the first time hiding. The same nurses and the same bed, as if Vicky hadn't been away at all. And it would surely be easier for the visitors who had been there before and wouldn't need directing again, and much easier for the family who preferred the quiet of the small ward and the perfect stillness of corridors and entrances here on Queen Square. But there wasn't anywhere to walk to, no offices filled with beautiful twenty-somethings and bars and shops to hold their attention – just a few too-quiet cafés and the main road crammed full of banks and print shops. There was the art school on the corner, but their summer show was still a couple of months away.

The family found another pub, a new one to try, just round the corner from Russell Square station it was perfect for picking up new, lost visitors who had been directed only that far. And they waited, but not in silence anymore – enough of that for now – and instead enjoyed being out and taking the opportunity to have conversations they hadn't really tried to before.

The word had got about and had managed to reach great distances over a few days with the help of no more than three old women and their telephones. The evening before had been taken up with lengthy exegeses, and the kind of groundless interpretation based on half-remembered gospel truths that made the word fitting. Old women calling every hour for updates when none could be given, yet in their head they came away with more information, more detail and best still ideas of what should be done. Amazing medical wisdom buried under years of cooking, cleaning and gossiping. A suburb full of walking witch doctors who pulled their children's teeth out with string and the slam of a door, sweated out colds with the help of electric blankets from Argos and could even tell the sex of an unborn child with a look at the mother from fifty paces – and of course what she was eating.

Vicky's eldest son remembered the time he had brought a girlfriend back for a family meal, the first and only one so far to have been chosen to attend one of these. She was handsome rather than pretty, heavy set and tall, with plump full breasts that worked well for her at fifteen, and a less appealing soft belly that they sat on when she took the weight off her legs. He had spotted her at school – after school in fact – at the first of the rehearsals held three times a week for two long terms to shape a two-hour musical planned for early summer. The hall had just been used for one of the modern-language exams the third years were forced to take and the desks were still neatly in lines across the front, three deep, with the main cast members sat in them as the chorus milled about behind. He was late and she was at the front, leaning forward slightly to rest her chest on the high desk to save her back. She looked like an old '50s siren to him even in a white shirt and thinning polyester blue pullover, the V coming down far enough to show the strain the shirt was under. He was transfixed, and surprised by the power of it all. They got talking afterwards under the pretext of discussing costumes and their parts, how best to learn their lines and who they thought might let the whole thing down. Like professionals, or not professional at all; whatever it was it seemed very important to be discussing things so seriously. And he couldn't help but think she might be interested because she was big too, and at least he stood as tall as she did, unlike so many of his friends still waiting for their elusive growth spurt. He hoped as they spoke that they might tacitly agree that they wouldn't be able to do better and it might work out. But before long they started talking about other things, who they fancied and what kinds of things they wanted to try out with those lucky few. Talking about experimentation without getting their hands dirty, like friends. And friends didn't do that kind of thing after getting on like that for a whole term and the holidays too, and so Vicky's eldest pulled the conversation back round again. All the while his eyes kept following the others, the prettier ones, around the hall and from the comfort of a couch later in the rehearsal run when he was invited over with a group of them to watch TV and talk about how it was going. But they would always prefer walking to the shops holding other people's hands, enjoying nonsense conversations or complete silence when the athletic boys were in a bad mood about not making it through to the county finals. He was learning where he fitted in quickly. And come the big night the two of them pulled it off remarkably well, taking control of the whole stage with the presence of their sheer size, whilst the others said their few lines quietly (some drunkenly) and clapped afterwards, self-congratulatory.

A week after their week of glory Vicky's eldest boy had invited his new friend to lunch with his parents and fragments of the extended family. Not to cement anything, he invited two other friends too, but they couldn't make it. But just as he had found himself six months before, none of his family could keep their eyes off every incredulous curve that threatened to engulf their five-foot frames without her noticing as she passed. Passed to the kitchen to help herself to the leftovers in cold greasy pyrex bowls filling the kitchen worktops – meaty chunks of fried beef and potatoes cooked with caramelised onions and garlic filling a large spoon and then her mouth, until the eldest aunt in the house stopped by her side on her way to the sink and patted her stomach whilst conferring judgement: a boy, definitely a boy. She left after that pretty quickly; a little afraid it was prophetic rather than taking offence.

Things like that happened in Vicky's house, with more of her family around her. Her children had learnt to try not to bring back anyone who mattered like girlfriends and boyfriends, although a stream of others had got quite used to it and could be found on occasion getting through large quantities of whisky and wine several hours after coming through the door in search of the younger generation, who weren't to be found. There was no escaping that quickly. No one left Vicky's house sober or without a good feeding. Looking like mad cows fattened for the slaughter, every last one, as they staggered home, full.

Over another small hill and a bigger one in the distance. Vicky kept the pace up and let the clean warm air fill her small lungs like a morning drag on a first fag when outside it's cold, cold, cold. Long ribbons of air reached down her throat, tickling her insides, clean shoes kicking up dust from the floor and her hair bouncing freely, getting in her eyes and being flicked back by a quick hand. And on top of the hill was a group of children to play with, dancing in a circle, holding hands, behind a tree with soft wisps of white blossom slowly creeping on to the thin winter branches. So she ran up to join them, but their circle was complete, with thirteen moving round with their heads at angles. One too many boys for the six girls, she thought, it should have been perfect. But they didn't see her, so she sat on the ground and waited, sitting patiently until the circle was broken as a boy left and came to join her, the others linking back and moving round still. He sat opposite and looked at her in silence with a crown of flowers as an offering for her head; two small hands reaching up and Vicky's head bending low in acceptance. And it was perfect: idyllic in the spring sun like an Italian painting, painted in the round, that she must have seen in a book. After all it was in a private collection now. And she sat like that for hours, holding still, knowing that an audience somewhere might be admiring each brushstroke and would notice the slightest twitch.

Vicky's younger son had been a bright boy, looking serious in dark suits when he was five. Her eldest son wore blue, her daughter pale pink. Standing in his aunt's garden with her husband's friends from the bank and their wives, he looked the perfect miniature Englishman: softly spoken, assured, but easily embarrassed. His uncle's colleagues looked at Vicky's children fondly and wanted to clap; like they had been trained specially for the occasion, the perfect trio for parties, weddings, barmitzvahs. Although they had not had a call about the last gig yet. Their speciality was the wedding anniversary – preferably very close family friends, feeling almost on home turf but not quite. The audience always showed a little more appreciation that way, didn't mind if they hit a bad note.

Vicky's children looked nothing like each other, even though there was only a year between each: Vicky's elder son taking after her, her younger boy her husband, and their daughter a very lucky and pretty combination of them both. And Vicky had been two inches taller than her husband before the shrinking started, and those genes in her eldest boy were pulled a little harder, with him stopping short of his seventeenth birthday to reach just over six feet. Not huge, but big enough for a family of short people. Even Vicky's friends had got it right, none of the closest circle being able to stand taller than her in her two-and-a-half-inch magenta heels, her favourite with a delicate T-bar strap.

But of course it was more than just size. That wouldn't have made for an interesting story, not war-

ranting more than a quick mention and a passing reference to a photo where one of them looked like he
had fought his way to the food first. To make them
seem irregular and mismatched. A comedy family, when
the comedy is about being disproportionate and gro-
tesque.

Once whilst on pilgrimage with their mother in
Belgium – the Holy Virgin having had a thing for
Western Europe for well over a century, right up to
a very '80s foray into the East – the boy's height had
caused some tension, when one of the other women
in the group had thought Vicky's eldest in a whole
other league, presuming he was watching his much
younger, almost baby, brother. Something that pleased
Vicky's elder boy at sixteen but made her younger son
puff himself up to increase his presence at fifteen. And
that was one to remember, at least for one of them.
With a single *Empire* magazine to share and re-read
over the long week (no cinema nearby to make use
of the good reviews), they should have known to have
brought more, or even a book, both bored already of
the one chip shop on the corner and the kiosk in the
hotel selling sweets for the little ones. No girlfriends
to call to sustain them during the week over a crackling line: voices bouncing up and back, through long
wires that hadn't been changed since the war. A very
strange place for two on the brink of becoming young
men – how lucky for their sister that she was off trek-

king for a Duke's medal with friends. A place cut off enough that the locals, as well as the phone lines, still felt the impact of the two great ones, with the long lists of the dead on plaques fixed to trees and still prominent in the middle of the forest where She had appeared to a twelve-year-old girl. A girl who, unlike all the others, had got married and had children – the eldest now keeping the souvenir shop just outside the gates thought appropriate when the Bishop of Liège gave his support in 1949.

But Vicky's younger son met someone that summer as the others prayed: his first proper girlfriend, hidden behind one of the huge conifers by the small chapel in the centre of the thick green. She had been brought by her mother too, a ferocious woman from Cork who lived in a house just a few streets from Vicky's, who was trying her hardest to make her prettiest daughter a little less pretty and a little more devout. After all, a real beauty was unlikely to give it all up to marry a God she hadn't seen. And they looked nothing like each other, in the way stout old Italian women look in comparison to the next generation – their presence enough to warn off men afraid of the changes sure to come.

Vicky's younger boy was too young to worry about things like that when the soft pink rounds of her cheeks looked so perfect it would have been sinful to imagine them with a single line, or sagging a little to give her jowls. She was in fact slightly plain, at least her prettiness was so well under wraps that not many of his friends at school had bothered to go looking for it. People would pass her on the street and be unaware, but in the middle of nowhere the blankness of disinterest on her face made Vicky's younger boy look, seeing a kindred spirit who would be pleased with the opportunity to have a conversation that didn't involve holy ghosts, horsemen and reformed prostitutes. Thank goodness for the lack of hotels. With just the three – and only one able to cater to old English speakers who would never dream of eating horse meat – she was bound to be spotted if he sat out front by the bar and waited, patiently.

Her mother already knew Vicky, being a regular pilgrim from the same large sandstone church, and having spent almost everything she earned – cleaning offices in the evenings and filling small stomachs with chips at St. Teresa's – on being the good pilgrim: Lourdes, an early April fixture, Banneax in the summer and Fatima late September. She had even made it as far as Mexico City to finally climb the steps up to the tiny chapel in Guadelupe on her knees after spotting where she was going on the Underground map with an icon's face in a box next to a toy horse that marked the next stop. Thankfully she had been leading the way, and did up the six tiers of stairs to the prize at the top too, never feeling it for a second with ample padding around each kneecap. And of course she made it home to Ireland every year, visiting Knock at the same time, if there was time.

Breda Kelly taught all three of her daughters well. Good girls, respected in the parish, all working hard, without a trace of ambition, softly spoken like Vicky's younger son and almost afraid to look up with each step taken between home and school. There certainly was no reason why Rita, her youngest and her best hope, needed to go further than that unless it involved a good deal of prayer and more bowed heads.

Rita must have taken after her father, Vicky's younger son thought, though no one had actually seen him for years, even knew what he did for a living. Only Rita's mother moved through the streets, scared the market traders for selling overpriced vegetables, and priests for not being pious enough or knowing the prayers she was taught as a girl – not like Father Eugene, whose memorial card took its place amongst loose change and bus tickets in her purse, to be carried around forever by his obedient followers. Groupies almost, and Vicky was one of them too, and so the connection grew. For a pious woman she cooked well, able to feed vast numbers without fuss or the luxury of a big budget and taste for indulgence. Vicky peeled the potatoes for her every Christmas as Breda made five small turkeys feed fifty of the parish's less than finest: old drunks from the streets and others from nearby homes who were rarely invited to sit at their own tables. For all everyone knew her own husband could have been amongst the crowd, but in the frenzy of activity – she could boss like a convent nun – she wasn't about to look up and make acknowledgements, and certainly never about to accept thanks. Everything a duty without even the smallest luxury enjoyed: her marriage, the children and her daily half hour break in front of the TV, as she played with the rosary ring on her left hand getting ready to put it to good use.

But back to Rita. She was short like her mother but half her size; small waist and chest, but one suspected a softer, rounder backside and thick hips. No one could have known for sure what lay beneath the knitted jumpers that draped down to just above the backs of her knees. Whilst Breda's hair was raven black Rita's was blonde – just – although she had missed out on her mother's ice-blue eyes, like a Pyrenean wolf hound and certainly as effective at keeping people away when used on guard. Rita's eyes were still blue, but softer, mixed with grey and green and flecks of hazel. Vicky's younger son liked to think they changed with the weather, though whether that actually happened was doubtful. More likely the light playing tricks, or her clothes bringing out one of the colours to make a match for him to admire.

Rita was good at school, but she was too artistic, her mother thought. But her maths was good, her writing neat and she was organised; perfect for the kind of job Breda wanted for her. If she had had boys she would only have wanted them to be good early risers and strong. Rita didn't have a chance. She had a small group of friends, all three a lot louder than her but sweet, letting her play, and in the corner of the playground she got a little louder herself and chatted and laughed at a great enough distance for no one else to hear. Even in class she sat at the back with the boys who liked to pretend they were far enough away not to take part in the lesson. But Rita was never moved to the front for any disturbance she caused and Vicky's younger son liked it there so he could see the board clearly without having to wear his brown plastic-framed glasses.

But it wasn't as if he had noticed her and sat away without anything to say. The girls he looked at were prettier – tetchy, stroppy madams who scared the local shopkeepers once the bell had rung and they poured out onto the street; finding the strength of woman-hood quickly and playing with it until it was unrec-ognisable as the first inklings of maturity. Skirts pulled up to show off thin pubescent legs and buttons on shirts undone to reveal the first curves beginning to erupt. Teasing and pulling them in and then making them look stupid, the boys loved it. And Vicky's younger son was part of the gang but slightly towards the back, not quite the first one to get picked but definitely not the last. Both Vicky's boys managed to maintain their ground precariously, caring about where they stood, the younger with the object lesson laid down by his brother in the year above. It was all like a spectator sport with only two small teams playing but the rest watching and living vicariously. And just like fat men on couches who shout at their favourites for missing a shot they could have got themselves surely, even drunk, all the boys lusted after just three girls and commented when their boyfriends got it wrong, not about to pay any attention to the lower divisions yet.

It was different when they were away. Vicky's younger boy could take a proper look before his friends noticed and passed judgement. Very adult indeed for a fifteen-year-old, even if he was just about to celebrate his birthday before the end of the summer. The start of the new year would change a few things – only half of the year were staying on to join the sixth form with most of the bad influences pleased instead to be up at seven, out the door and obedient when it counted at work. Two of the prettiest gone too to look after babies with their mothers' help just after the year had sat their GCSEs. And they hadn't done too badly at all. The boys had caught up with the girls, who were happy too that they didn't tower over them all anymore. The loud ones were still there shouting, joined by a few new faces who had made it up the table and been promoted to the new league. Vicky's younger son wasn't one of the biggest movers but he had made a little ground, he would have to make a more concerted effort after this next set of exams he thought, and on to university.

Demanding a small concession to their new-found maturity, the school had allowed the sixth formers, who wanted to, to smoke on the defunct concrete tennis court tucked behind the main building and sunken into the ground. It was perfect for keeping them out of sight of parents and governors. The only other time it was used was for the annual photo. No chance of a quick game with eighty pairs of smoke-filled lungs loitering about the baseline. Vicky's younger boy didn't smoke. He was taking Biology, Chemistry and Maths ready to start four years at UCL studying Chemical Engineering as soon as the brown envelope came through with all the right letters. Rita had chosen English, Art and French in readiness for nothing in particular, so no chance of them bumping into each other in class. Thank goodness for the miraculous match-making powers of their mothers' Blessed Virgin.

The thing was that Rita did believe, liking the idea of believing anyway, and toyed with it, not knowing there was anything else to believe in. All whilst her friends watched the boys from their corner in the playground, seeing some kind of beautiful choreography in their gauche, laddish movements. But once Rita started talking that was enough for her at least – nothing in particular to focus on that could possibly be interesting; certainly not seeing all the things her friends' magazines kept saying she should be searching out. Just like that; an old head on a young body or perhaps both of them young and not quite at the point the others were at yet. It was clear her small group would get bored of her quickly, and sure enough by the time they had turned seventeen she was almost left talking to herself completely, the difference never registering itself on her face – as if she had been talking like that the whole time anyway, just with the luxury for a few years of being able to speak the words out loud, but very softly.

Vicky's younger son had always had his own group too but wasn't afraid to join the others kicking a ball about the uneven concrete; the towers from the paint factory next door casting shadows for posts that were only the right distance apart by the time it got to afternoon break in May. By the time his A levels had started and he had moved to the sixth-form buildings with the rest – joining his brother and taking Rita with him – the only uneven playing field was taken up by the other students smoking. But by that time he didn't miss the football too much and soon found another way to get involved; with drinks bought from the pub down the hill with a landlord who pretended not to notice when his staff served the ones they shouldn't. It would just have knocked their confidence, Terry liked to think.

Vicky's eldest came from the same drinking family too, of course, and had seen years of hard practice, but it wasn't about that for him then; rather he could buy Imogen – a pretty red-haired girl who liked to look moody and write sad songs while she smoked badly rolled joints – a Pernod and black, which she could sip slowly like treacle and thank him for later. But Vicky's younger son never got anywhere with girls like that. He just wasted the money he earned on Saturdays working at Cromwell's on the high street folding and selling jeans. Seeing Rita through the trees he suddenly realised he had been going at it all wrong.

And so he made the decision to change his plan.

Within the next three days, before they left for home, he struck something up with a few short conversations and came home with a girlfriend. Although Vicky didn't know and still didn't after their being together for almost two years – Rita afraid her mother would find out from her and Vicky's younger son too discreet to think it anyone's business. A strange couple sitting on the side and bringing out each other's shyness, when their coupling could have made people sigh. The boys at school would have made fun first, of course. And that was very important too, neither sure they'd be able to take that.

In the end – as people always want to know – nothing very much came of it. Rita started at Reading where she could stay with an aunt, and Vicky's younger son found a place in halls on Pentonville Road, buying a desk and some lever arch files in preparation for all the work still ahead of him. And neither wanted to make too much of a fuss, and so saw less and less of each other, beginning to forget what they had filled the previous two years with. They wrote letters for a while – the pages seeming so expansive to fill they spoke on the phone instead, and planned to meet. And they did for a drink on Christmas Eve; a vodka and orange and a lager top sipped together as their families waited expectantly for the big day the next morning. But with so little to say and the realisation that they had even misremembered each other's face, they left their drinks half finished. And the walk towards home together was just as hard to stomach, quickly passing old friends who had gathered for similar reunions, their small talk about new things impossible to recall when either looked back.

Vicky certainly would have sighed if she had known. She would have loved to see another of her children married, and for Vicky two dates had potential, let alone two years. But she couldn't complain, no one vying for her place and distracting either of her boys from rallying around when she called. And imagine if she had come over to stay. Where would she have slept?

★   ★   ★

Vicky wasn't thinking like that now and was ready for some proper excitement, and some direction.

The day had started up again, the stillness of sitting bent forward having made a mess of her lower back. Still no dancing for her in the circle and the crown of flowers didn't look so good when she actually had it on her head.

She was beginning to feel detached from what was going on around her. If not for that one boy she was sure the others wouldn't have even seen her, dancing as they were, so content with themselves. Like they were all there in this space together but were unable to see anything that wasn't their own. That made her think. She had seen three people already she recognised and she probably *had* met that boy too, but it was he who had remembered her and not the other way round. She didn't worry too much trying to place him, not annoyed at herself for forgetting. It was almost like when she was at home and older, stuffed into slim carriages on the Northern line, taking her from Euston to Goodge Street with the same people who refused to make eye contact. Even after years of the same faces. Not very neighbourly at all – she would have talked back if the right kind of person had spoken to her, one of the old ladies perhaps or the young men in new suits who reminded her of her sons' friends.

She started to think hard about the others she might

be able to find. Her little sister Lucy at the top of her list and old friends from home she wasn't too sure would be here or not. It had been such a long time and no one ever phoned to let her know how they were getting on. And she had kept her number the same to make it easy for people to keep in touch, never thinking to take it out of the directory either.

Vicky had no idea where to start looking for Lucy. She could imagine her sitting on the ground with grass poking up through the gaps of one outstretched leg with the other bent round in a triangle, a large clean pad of thick cream paper propped up and pencils scattered around by her side, a red one pinning up a knot of her hair to keep it up and out of the way. She always had loved drawing and would have found a view worth the while putting down on paper and held still. But apart from the dancing children on the hill Vicky hadn't seen anywhere that looked like the picture in her mind: sweeping meadows and a clean, pale English sky, freckled with clouds, like the one that sat above the Heath the first day they had seen it together.

At every turn the sky was different, just like the trees, and if she had to pass through a jungle to get to a wood she was ready and able, and more than capable of finding her way through instinct alone. But she hadn't yet had to do battle and after her early readiness she hadn't felt the need since to put the fear of God into anyone. And she knew that just wouldn't do if she was going to get to where she was going.

In her mind she started to picture it all: a dragon perhaps or maybe some kind of knight on horseback, weighed down with heavy armour and a very unnecessary flag to stake claims wherever he went. Now either one of those would be perfect, and could quite justify a little dirty fighting. Below-the-belt kind of stuff, or maybe a trap – a hole dug deep and covered with twigs, for a trip and fall and a good week without food until they were done for. Savouring the taste of doing it all for the right reason, she couldn't wait to start, feeling the frustration of doing nothing building.

Back in the hospital Vicky was making a fuss. Kicking up her sheets and growling at the nurses who cleaned her mouth with a suction tube. Just like a baby refusing to understand that medicine is good for it, or a dog not about to accept the necessities of soap and water, preferring instead to run in the park and get even dirtier, heart pumping hard and free in the good company of others, chasing sticks flying through the air.

With that Vicky started running, realising she hadn't bothered to before, trying to shake the feeling. And it had been an awfully long time since she had been able to move that fast. Her small feet, attached to skinny legs, hit the ground and made little mushrooms of dust spring up, caught and projected through the air with the long rays of the sun behind each, and her heart beat faster, flushing her face and making her lungs work to keep her body going forward. What a feeling – of being in control enough to choose her course and feel like she could go on forever, her mind paying no heed to her body, which was showing the signs that it would only go so far. All as simple as that for the time being. Her decision to start and hers to stop. She must have run miles, jumping over small ponds of rain water that collected where they shouldn't have and down and up through shallow ditches. She still felt she could keep going but she came to water – a beautiful twisting river, impossible to vault, that obviously led somewhere important. Someone's way of telling her that was enough. And she didn't want to cross it anyway, she wanted to get to where it was going, using the water to carry her so she could rest. Of course there was a small boat left aground on the bank with all the paint wiped clean off – made for two, but perfect for one who wanted to stretch out and feel the sun on her face.

What a way to see it all, at least a good slice of the action. The river looked like a two-lane highway; the water going in different directions on either side, like the steady flow on the Van Wyck before six and the proper rush for the airport. Her American friend Leslie from the office had told her about all this; regaling her with tales of missing planes and hair-raising journeys back and forth to JFK, dodging the traffic, wishing she had taken Queens Boulevard instead.

Looking left (the way she'd be going if she got on this side) she saw that it curled to the right, hiding what was further off in the distance of a bend. The boat was steady on the ground and she easily climbed over the side and in, to take her place on the bench – just a set of worn thin planks – towards the bow. First she had to make sure there were no holes. No point starting an adventure like this without due care, and spotting a couple she fished about in her pockets to find something to stop them up. All she had was a clean white hankie and a warm, softened wine gum – it must have got stuck in her pocket from before – which she eyed closely and tried to blow off the fluff stuck to it. She forced each one into the holes and sat back proudly. That would have to do, and of course it did. And besides she didn't like the yellow ones anyway.

But now she would have to get out again and push the boat into the water and hop in before it moved off. She hadn't thought of that and sighed, feeling lazy with the thought. Why wasn't there anyone to help when she needed them? Before she moved she took a good look around, but no one in sight, no one at all. So she got up and out, over the side, which seemed lower than before, shrinking to fit, and onto the bank again to push. Putting her back into it she shifted it with one sharp action, the water standing still long enough for her to get in without a problem, rocking and holding the hard belly of the boat with the control of two large hands. How obedient, Vicky thought. If she had wanted to get over to the other side she didn't doubt the water would have parted for her to cross. But enough of that – she wasn't interested in over there – much better to see what was round the bend and then decide when to jump out.

The water picked up and started moving her forward at a pace. The shores cleared and opened out to fields with far-off buildings – flat grey stone, tall leaded windows and even a few turrets – sitting at the end of each, not budging after centuries of sitting still. The boat moved along in fits and starts, and Vicky slipped down from her bench and curled herself up in a blanket she had pulled from underneath, not wanting to look behind her and see if she was in fact being propelled by a young man with a long wooden pole topped with a straw boater. The tourists might always take pictures but she wanted to enjoy the view. And anyway, she didn't have a camera, she didn't think.

Under bridges and people passing overhead. Vicky waved but they went on their way, all carrying books as she imagined they would do, never having seen any of this before. First past Queens', then King's, Caius, Trinity and St. John's. Amazing how she got the order right. And the bridges changed shape seeming to get older the further she went, but she couldn't have known that for sure. A very old institution straddling an even older river, taking control and making it its own. But this was all in her head, and as she passed further along it began to clear to reveal what she was actually after. The beginning of the revelation anyway, where the images sat real in front of her rather than coming from a moment's thought, a memory of something she had seen herself or heard talk about.

But enough of that for now. Vicky had to have a good look for herself first.

The time at The Middlesex had felt like a break for the family, a time to let their minds wander and think back and forward. In a place like that everyone looked sick, but nothing too life-threatening. More a case of dying of pneumonia or a bug picked up from the dirty floors. Nothing happened too quickly in the old wards up eight flights, the nurses trained to take good care whilst the doctors peddled old but trusted drugs and messed around with ancient tools of the trade: the stethoscope they had received from their parents when they qualified and probes held together at the base with peeling masking tape. It was much more like a care ward for the ones who couldn't be expected to go on anymore, without anyone too young to make you feel it was tragic. But when the family had looked closer they realised they had been wrong – the man who had been opposite Vicky had a four-year-old son, but a grandfather's face, after months of illness eating into the muscles that should have held his skin taut and carried his eyes flush in their sockets. All this with the soft skin of a fleshy face hanging down, without furrows in a brow to prop it up a little.

But the days had passed quickly enough for Vicky there and whilst the nurses had kept watch the doctors had worried. No stop to the trickle of blood and only the briefest signs that her mind was still worth saving. It was like one of her husband's cost-analysis sheets with rows and columns with numbers, padded out with zeros, and a final ruling – the number that helped the managers decide whether it was all worth it after all. But they had had to have a team full of number-crunchers in place for years to keep them in ideas, and the action itself surely shouldn't have cost all that.

So back at The National the family continued to sit by Vicky's bedside, worried by the extra attention, the newer equipment. Watching her hard, reading into the slight movements, her eldest caught a glimpse of what was going on in her head, when her right eye opened late on Friday to take in the view. She must have realised almost immediately that it wasn't as good as the one she had spread out in front of her, even with her sons framing the left-hand side, her daughter and husband on the right, all peering in to fill the picture. Then black, and then some colour again.

Chapter Five

Lying on the banks, stretched out in the sun, was a large dragon. Vicky got the feeling she might have almost arrived. Thick skinned and worn like expensive leather left out in the dry heat or scuffed from too many airport conveyor belts. A mix between dull grey and dark brown, polished in places with natural bumps and ridges, without the need for the metal studs of a Chesterfield; smoke rising in curls from lungs the size of whole children, as the wind tickled shoots of hair creeping out of a large flat nose. Just like an old cat on the hearth of the meadow, and just as ready to jump up, stretch and pounce, Vicky thought. Or an old man. She had known a few with a little too much spirit.

But Vicky wasn't afraid, feeling able enough here to give St. Joan a lesson in battling. The armour would be under the seat, she knew, and a good choice of weapon to slay the prey. But it was almost like she couldn't be bothered; a nonchalant knight working for the cause. The way it should be. After all, only madmen actually enjoyed the fight. And little boys trapped in hairy, foul-smelling bodies on Saturday nights when she liked to stay in. All that just wasn't her thing so she took a breath and smelled the faintest trace of Chanel, her daughter's favourite, wafting around her, there to keep her fresh and cool in the morning light, whilst her heart started beating hard and a glow came on.

The boat came to a slow stop. Urging her to get out and spill some blood, when she hadn't decided she'd need to do that. She would have to get a closer look first, look into its eyes and then make a decision. Eyes always gave it away and a close inspection might even reveal a kind soul. The hop onto the bank was easy enough, not even a small splash to get her wet. Now if that had been true the boat would have run aground, and the stop would have been anything but slow and easy. But she liked it better this way.

Vicky walked up and looked at her nails, painted pink, as she did, shrugging her shoulders under the weight of a metal vest, and an even heavier sword slung over her shoulder. She could have held it well enough in her hands, but it was pulling her around to the right, like her satchel on the way to school filled with too many books. A room full of twisted spines and sore necks – her granddaughter would have it easy with a miniature rucksack that matched her trainers.

Her nails were perfect. Short, but painted beautifully. She was so busy caught up in admiration that she walked straight into the round of his belly with a bang, without the fleshiness to break the collision, as good fat ought to. She placed her hands flat on the skin and spread them out. Left and right together, to span as much as she could do, although the span, centred about her tiny chest, didn't reach very far. What she felt was huge and distended, hardly likely to have the sensitivity to feel anything – particularly two small hands and a tiny ear pressed up to hear the rumblings.

The warmth heated her cheek like a pillow in the morning, or a firm chest at night. Quite soft too like the wing of a library chair, propping up a head focusing too hard on the words to concentrate on keeping itself held aloft. She wanted to rest for a while and, without really thinking, she let her eyes close and was soothed to sleep with the movement of air, filling a lung and then exhaled, with the perfect rhythm of water lapping. And now for a cocktail, as she imagined the sun setting in Greece. It wasn't the wisest thing she could have done, really stupid in fact; falling asleep on the job could have been dangerous, and a quicker beast could have swallowed her whole without waking her or disturbing its own sleep very much. But when Vicky did finally open her eyes she had one the size of a human head (fully grown at that) peering back at her. And from the shiny and slimy black of an old eye, she could tell she was safe – and there would certainly be no need to use her sword. Maybe she could leave it on the ground now, it would only get heavier. Looking harder and getting closer Vicky couldn't quite make out what the beast was thinking, and she knew conversation would be useless – large animal, small brain – but his soft, lazy eye was transfixing, so she stopped still, and stopped thinking about her own discomfort, just for a short while at least.

With Vicky awake, the animal's interest picked up a little, his pupil dilating to get more light in to bring her into focus. He must have thought her part of his stomach before, not quite sure *that* had been there before, and certainly no likeness could be found on the other side when he had checked to be sure. Perfect confusion for a stupid animal who hadn't the inclination to spend time getting to know his own body better – lumps and bumps from old fights and dried mud and grass; even parts of braches that hadn't moved out the way frequently got stuck to him, in the crevices of rough skin, and pressed into the softness of his belly when he had remained flat on the ground, asleep for too long. But those things never moved, or made sounds, and those that did didn't stand calmly by looking back at him. With her not being bothered, he wasn't going to do a thing, pleased he hadn't scared another one off. It got quite lonely being frightening, and under the massive expanse of his body was nothing more than a timid creature, happy to eat the rest up when he was hungry, but usually more content pushing his head into thickets of plump, fleshy grass. More often than not the taste of flesh made him nauseous, even after a lick of his fire's breath had charred it well enough to be unrecognisable. A little like Lennie without George to tell him to play nicely, he was more likely to break a spine by sitting down awkwardly or by stroking too hard with his body against another, trying hard to start purring.

Vicky was agile enough, with her slight and nimble six-year-old frame, to escape if she saw his body descending above her to hit the floor fast. And she would be able to tickle him under the chin without feeling the need to pet him too much; all for her pleasure not his, without a large maze of delicate nerve endings working to carry back the feeling of her tiny fingers. You can spoil pets like that anyway, she always thought, and could throw the cat off her lap without remorse if his padding got uncomfortable or boring.

And what an odd couple! She liked the thought of people looking at them strangely, unsure how it worked and who was boss, when she knew that she was, of course. The idea of it made her smile, although from the look in his eyes he could take or leave the arrangement Vicky was hatching. She hadn't even told him what she had decided, but that had always worked quite well with her husband, and for all her friends too, whose old men had the same look of apathy spread languidly over their tired faces. He would go along with her, as long as she pretended to keep his pace, if only because he didn't quite know what else was on offer, what he had been doing over the years to keep him occupied before she even came along.

And with the expertise of an elephant handler, she got him to move with a gentle prod, coaxing him to roll over a little so he was sitting square. With a sharper strike with her elbow he began to raise himself off the floor, taking his weight on four broad feet, lifting up only three feet so his body still hung just a fraction above the ground. She knew she'd have to be careful where they walked if she didn't want him sweeping things along she didn't want him to. Her own small body included. Muscles flexed and tendons tightened to help take the strain and Vicky looked on, a little unsure she had chosen the right model. She should have got a newer one, she thought, one with a little more speed and agility. But it was like getting a battered MG to drive around town in, much better than a new one, and a lot easier to get hold of with a fist full of notes at seventeen; nail marks on the steering wheel telling of boy racer manoeuvres before they had become the mainstay of little town squares, and touched-up paintwork, faded all over by rain and air.

Now she knew this old creature wasn't a car, though full-on he looked like Vicky's first, a much cherished

Beetle. He certainly wasn't going to be any help saving her legs – it would have taken too long to get him to sit back down and for her to clamber up to the peak of his back. So what use was he going to be? She did begin to wonder, seeing how slow he was and how he lacked direction. But partners were sometimes like that, and now the decision had been made, it was her job to walk by his side and make sure they took the path together. Vicky knew her husband would have been a little more sprightly.

And as you do with the kind of old people who aren't in fact much use, have no good stories to tell, and don't do too well being kindly, well-mannered and wise, she started to look a bit closer to see something that would endear him to her. He was quite sweet really. The tragedy of seeing what once must have been a fearsome sight reduced to this tugged at her sympathy, and she could see that any care she could give might bring a little reward. But he needed a name, for he hadn't had the energy to speak yet and she couldn't very well speak to him, until he deigned to utter his first words, without one. Just like the pressure of naming a baby and hoping it lives up to the label and extremely painful to watch when you name a stout ugly one Isabella, or a willowy future society princess Maud – not that Vicky had heard a small child called that for many years. It was much better to think of him as a pet, and call him Rex. No one would get hurt by that, she thought. And it was a fitting choice too, matching the regal roots in her own and honouring her favourite snake-hipped singer too. And so the conversations started. Even about how she had come up with his name. About Teresa from work who had tried for seven years for a baby without success, and so made a vow in church to call her first-born Mary on Vicky's insistence it would help, if she said a novena each night too. But Teresa had had a boy, and he was baptised as promised, although none of his friends found out about that until the day he had to bring his passport to school for the annual day trip to France. She assumed he had had it changed by deed poll now; after all he did like going away and a reluctance to show his passport would have only raised suspicion at Immigration.

Rex looked over from time to time, waiting for a few of Vicky's streams of thought to wash over him. The way she jumped from one to another, then back again, without any perceptible link would have made his neck hurt if he craned round each time to reassure her he was listening. At the speed she was going he wouldn't have been able to keep up anyway, and it would have been worse, like he was just looking over for no real reason, getting the timing wrong. Better to stare straight ahead, he thought, giving the impression he was concentrating hard. Vicky didn't mind. A less than attentive audience was usually better than none.

What an odd couple they did make: walking and talking, as if they knew where they were going, the small leading the mighty, when in fact they hadn't a clue.

Outside the back entrance of the National Hospital was a bench, in pale beech, with eighty-eight cigarette stubs around it. Eighty-nine – Vicky's eldest added his own. She had been back here for three days now and he had found this place to sit and wait, ready and at hand but a little distanced from the action. The area backed out on to a wing of Great Ormond Street and between the murals, spied through large '30s windows, he heard the odd cry, and wasn't sure if a child was in pain or being forced to laugh by the clowns they brought in through the week. Some of the doctors wore red noses too, but not when they operated.

They had used the space there to shoot a scene in *Sliding Doors* when Gwyneth sees her man kissing his ex and runs off thinking the worst, waiting for the rain to start before an explanation and the revelation on a beautiful, old, metalwork bridge; hair wet and a mess but still looking beautiful in the moonlight. A short run for a long way and the day passing too quickly – the relevant licences in London being hard to get to ensure continuity. He didn't realise that till much later, after he watched the film for the eighth time, but even then as he sat and smoked another cigarette he thought there was something special about the place, a feeling of calm, even though it was the newest bit, latched on ten years before and opened by the Princess Royal. Clean and bright but not any architectural delight, just new red brick and steel, the rest painted white. Not very special at all, and getting dirtier with his help – just a drive for ambulances and none ever came. That must be a good sign, at The National.

Kicking up all those butts, after having located and displaced his own, Vicky's eldest looked around for a face but there weren't any. So a voice would have to do. His phone could be switched on, now outside and no chance of interference, and he thought what it might have been like if he hadn't had one to use. Who would talk to him on demand if it wasn't for all that technology wrapped up into a small piece of black plastic and metal? He would have been forced to become one of those men who repeatedly accost tourists and students and first time WestEnders who don't know better than to talk back.

Dialling and waiting, three rings, and Emily was on the other end hatching plans for the summer, the perfect diversion. A bit of work first and then some travelling, but they didn't have backpacks and might have to go and stay with her aunt in France instead. He'd have to call his temping agency and find out if they had got anything that would pay well enough so he could get the money together. Vicky had got him a prime place there with their pushiest of agents a long time back, roasting more chickens for one of her friend's daughters. She had been brought up vegetarian by parents and coveted the taste, and had gone on to join Adecco on Oxford Street. She had always been good on the phone and was even better at keeping the best- paid jobs for her favourites. Vicky knew keeping her fed on roast meat would pay off one day, even if she had had to do it in secret.

The last job hadn't gone so well, but Vicky's eldest didn't feel too bad remembering how he had had nothing to do in the one before that anyway. And all this was a very good excuse, much better than the time he had stayed at a friend's flat in West Hampstead and had got locked in by an unknown flatmate with no escape through the third-storey windows. Feeling guilty as he called and said he wouldn't be able to make it today, though the lack of food had served as punishment enough: three boiled sweets in a tin like the ones old couples keep in their glove compartment and half a stale bagel before he was rescued at lunch-time. But Emily kept speaking sweetly and brought him back. Her parents were praying hard, even the monks at Ampleforth – her father had a few good connections – and between them all at least that was covered, all would go as it was meant to. And that was what he couldn't figure out. Now he knew it was the kind of argument that filled whole books and lives, but it hadn't seemed to make the flock pause and think. If it was all part of a plan, and it was going to happen anyway, what was the point of praying? He, of course, had started to himself.

He felt guilty thinking that. His mother wouldn't be proud this time. Even though he hadn't felt bad about a whole lot of things recently the doubt and pause to question would have made him feel sinful at fourteen when he still went for Mass in the library during perfectly good lunch breaks every Tuesday, with just four others and the nun who taught them German. But it was good to hear things he should have been saying himself. Things his mother would want him to say, that prayers were being said and candles lit across London and further afield. Never mind what the doctors were saying and what his sister had found out about on the Internet – about a pioneering surgeon in New York, who had a great house on Long Island. Vicky's eldest was wondering whether, if his mother could speak, she would be as resistant to the medical thinking on offer and look so hard elsewhere. Not her style at all, but then again there's nothing like being scared. And he thought he might have caught sight of it in her eyes the other day. Or it was nothing, just her lying there fast asleep with her eyelids slightly open. Who could possibly tell?

The wait continued. More people upstairs. So he sat

and unpeeled the gold line on the plastic wrap of his cigarettes. Sliding off the two transparent cases, opening the top and pulling the foil, scrunching it together with the tips of his fingers and tying it back round with the opening thread. Then into the bin. He could do with another one now, just thinking of the relief: what to do with hands and face when there's nothing to do at all. But the words kept coming so there wasn't time for that now, especially since he had been joined by some of the visitors; 'uncles' he hadn't seen for years, and their children who had grown so much he couldn't help but stare at the chest on the eldest even though he wasn't really interested.

They all smoked with him. Pointless conversations about inhaling, ridiculous duty, and the benefits of rolling your own followed. And the questions about what he was doing now: does it pay well? Ah, the Internet, that's the way to go. Vicky's eldest wasn't sure about that, thinking how little work he had got so far, but they all seemed happy nonetheless, and he didn't want to spoil any sense of mutual understanding.

Vicky's new insistence on keeping her eyes firmly shut had made things difficult. The visitors had started to come to see her family instead, to see how they were doing, catch up on what they had been up to and then leave. It was as if they had come for a chat at the wrong time and found Vicky resting, feeling they mustn't disturb the ill as they recuperate. Not their fault at all, but it made the youngsters see how it worked when things like this happened, and how they had a better idea of what to say: the twenty-something cousins listening carefully before starting an appropriate question, nervously but with some understanding, to the doctors who addressed them first. It must be all the drama on TV. Good moral and medical lessons in life, the dialogue easy to recall and giving them a taste of the language of a place like this, whilst their parents had shuffled papers and worked towards pensions. No travelling for them to broaden the mind, just coach tours around Italy after years of saving, and very few new books. Even the news came and passed without excessive, learned comment. No *Observer* readers amongst them. The age of enlightenment had come and passed them by, with rules of sophistication and wide-eyed open-mindedness.

It seemed political. An illegitimate post-colonial baby, looking so remarkable it could have passed for the real thing, but not quite. Now, Vicky's children knew that their aunts and uncles needed more of an explanation – just in the way all fresh adults think the older ones out of touch – but when they couldn't understand the basics of human anatomy, learnt at ten usually (surely?), the gaps in their knowledge fissured further to form chasms: open and airy and so inexplicably big, all those who peered over the side were left magnificently, breathlessly silent. Vicky would have known to keep her mouth shut, happy letting the children talk their talk whilst she prayed for some clarity of thought for them. No mixing the two, she knew what she was good at.

Rex had become a little quicker. The blood had finally found every last inch of his body and Vicky could pick up the pace without fearing she would leave him behind. She could hear them over her and she knew she didn't have that long to get there. If she tried to say something back she'd have to stop and make the effort. And she didn't feel she could do that just now.

She wanted a collar for Rex, and that was all she could think about for the moment. A studded leather one would have been perfect, but unless she killed and skinned a cow and cured its hide she wasn't sure whether she'd get it just the way she wanted. She could always pluck one out of the air – and that could happen here – but as yet nothing had appeared in her hand and she wasn't sure whether she should start searching about for an alternative. Keeping a good lookout, Vicky kept on walking, almost silent now with concentration. She ran ahead and to the left and right, rooting under bushes, running back empty-handed. Finally she saw it, under a tree, wrapped and buckled at the base, exactly the same size as his fat, fleshy neck.

She ran ahead again as soon as she spotted it, knowing she'd have trouble getting it loose and hauling it back. The leather was stiff and new, and it took all her strength, holding tight to the loop framed by the silver buckle and leaning back with her weight. Finally she had it free and in her hands and spun about to face Rex head on – the look of satisfaction on her face doing nothing to enliven the look on his. And if she had been standing directly in front of him, without the sturdy tree behind her to plump her out, she didn't doubt that he wouldn't even have stopped, ploughing right through her now his slow momentum had got going. But having stopped and realising he wouldn't hear the end of it, he sat back down, bent his head forward and let her lasso his neck; once and twice and then a third and successful time, whilst he made himself too comfortable again. Once on, Vicky was in control. She liked to think. Whether he wanted to continue to sit or sleep was of no interest to her, and with the lead from the collar held securely in her hands she could get him to go where she wanted, and when. He didn't have the energy to disagree.

The two marched on. One focused on putting one foot in front of the other without losing the beat, and the other on where they were heading. With her to lead, there was no doubt about it. She'd have to figure it out soon, or she'd be found out. No one likes being led down the wrong road; however stupid they are, they always figure it out. And she remembered the time she had pretended to know where Warwick Avenue tube was, leading eight of them up Harrow Road instead. Not a very long walk from Royal Oak but everyone soon noticed when they had come round full circle and had to go a different way.

That walk was so long ago no one could remember it clearly. There was still some talk about times like that though, a pub here and picnic there, the time Vicky's cousin Christopher had got lost on the way to the woods and was so angry with himself that he refused to eat any of the sandwiches his wife had made. Silly, when they all tasted so good. Then there was the time in Spain.

Two families packed into a camper van, doing their European tour, through France to Spain, on to Portugal and back. They had to cross thousands of miles in fifteen days and be back in time to start work on Monday. And they managed to just do it too, with only a few hours to spare, having seen very little apart from camping sites and visa offices, after one of the group had forgotten they'd be going through Spain twice and needed more papers. And it was hot. The youngest, Vicky's daughter, and the eldest, Christopher's mother-in-law, couldn't cope, and the thought of coming home to cooler air raced through their minds from the second day. It must have been dehydration.

Christopher's wife had brought a palette of cream soda from a cash-and-carry in Leytonstone, but after a day in the 40° van, the sickly syrup had thickened and lost its bubbles. There were even a few left when they got back, which she had never expected, and her son had a week of taking them to school with his packed lunch. After that the two families started going away by themselves, taking planes instead, or staying closer to home when they couldn't afford that.

Even the weekend parties stopped, when the older children in the group drank upstairs and the adults danced with each other in Christopher's or Vicky's living room to the sounds of Boney M and *D.I.S.C.O.* By 2 o'clock in the morning, once the drink had fully taken hold, they played soppier ones, miming whilst they danced, tying yellow ribbons and knocking three times in the air.

Christopher was very proud of his record collection and didn't like making copies to share; dancing instead with pride at the good choices he had made and collected, stamping his right foot, marking out the beat of whatever he was moving to with short sharp claps. All the while his mother-in-law looked after the younger ones, bounced the smallest on her knee and put her, Vicky's daughter, under the dining table with a blanket to sleep so no one would stand on her head as they danced – just until she was old enough to join her cousins upstairs to sip lager from cans.

What a way to spend the weekends. Even Christopher's mother-in-law enjoyed it a little, especially in the morning when she could get up first, walk over the children, scattered in the living room wrapped in sheets and sleeping bags, and start cooking in the kitchen – making the perfect hangover cure for her very extended family. And then off to Mass.

She didn't make it to see Vicky but lit candles and prayed, talking to her priest after Sunday service to get the best deal. How many Hail Holy Queen's to see her all right, she asked, were there any new novenas he had heard about and were any other parishioners off to Lourdes for a Mass to be arranged at the Basilica for a small donation? But her daughter and one of her grandchildren came together, both looking older than Vicky's children remembered; it had been a while. Angie still with long black hair, she looked the same from behind, but her face looked tired, though still pretty for a woman well into her fifties. Not enough parties to keep it fresh, or simply the sadness of having to make a visit like this when there would be no chance for a catch-up over coffee. That holiday had done a lot of damage.

Vicky's sisters had kept a vigilant guard, coming in the fifteen miles together like children going to camp, holding onto plastic bags and each other's hands and looking lost after misremembering which way garden squares faced and where the landmarks used to be.

Now if they hadn't got their bearings from their old favourites — open-windowed cafés serving cake, and clothes shops all now closed — they would have been fine. But the routes were well worked out now after a week, though the move from one hospital to the other and then back did cause confusion, as they came up from the Underground and forgot which way to turn in the crowd that spewed out with them.

When the girls were little they liked to pick favourites from the group. But there were seven, so three pairs and one left out, but not for long as the fights that came made shuffling the reserve vital. Vicky was one of the smallest and liked the idea of getting into trouble, taking someone along only if they served a good purpose, to hold ladders and keep watch. But they always told on her, so she had to keep changing her favourite, the lucky recipient always afraid when that happened that trouble lay ahead. Like the time she hid a gecko in her mother's slipper, covering the opening with the other, to keep it in until it was called upon to play its part perfectly.

But it was different now. Vicky hadn't been in trouble with anyone like that for years. And she had grown a lot quieter, preferring to be mischievous from her own home, giggling to herself rather than to any audience. Still defiant: at 3 in the morning, coming downstairs to watch old films and drink rum and Coke, ordering takeaway Chinese on a new credit card when she had finished cooking a loin of pork and roast potatoes for the family, and slipping to William Hill to join the old men during the afternoon when she should have been at home resting from work, sick with another mysterious stomach cramp. A peculiar way for a woman like her to fill up the days leading to retirement, but it kept her busy, and the walks to the high street fit. After all, she enjoyed drinking and smoking and all the things that went with both, and if the others hadn't been so disapproving she wouldn't even have needed to feign a logic that led her to insist, 'I only buy the odd packet of ten.' She in fact kept to twenties. It worked out cheaper that way.

And while she watched afternoon TV on days like that she practised in the kitchen, finding new ingredients and discovering how to make old recipes taste better. She had a letter from the doctor giving her some sick leave, and now that it was official – no thrill in skiving, of lurking about her house with the pleasure of getting away with it – she wasn't happy if she didn't play the housewife a bit. Good for when she wasn't joining friends after Mass to collect money and organise coffee mornings for CAFOD. And she kept a lookout for people in need of feeding up at a more local level, even when they protested, and could have in fact done with a good run instead. It was a perverse logic. The less they asked, the more they got, piled high on mismatched plates, that were brought out one at a time to the living room, to sit perched on awkward laps at an angle. So she could recline again and get them talking to her, knowing they were here to stay for a little while longer.

Vicky's curries were legendary, a perfected art that shone for all to see and try to emulate like light in a Vermeer. At the start of each weekend the neighbours would knock on the door carrying large pots of chicken for her to transform and pass back over the fence for a feast that lasted till Sunday night. The last dregs were the tastiest as the oven-roasted spices settled in, eaten slowly in front of ceramic experts on the *Roadshow*, watching closely, hoping to spot something hidden in the attic with the same expectation they had had the night before focused on coloured balls whirling in a glass sphere. She knew what each of them liked, making things hot for the O'Mearas at 36 and easier to swallow for the Franks at 32. Even the choice of meat was perfect, with Vicky giving precise instructions before they made their way to the butcher's on Friday. Tom next door only liked chicken breast off the bone, left in large pieces, bubbling away in a pale, orangey gravy. That caused problems. Every time Vicky cooked for anyone she took a cut to feed the family. And her husband liked small knuckles of darker meat, in a thick pungent sauce that would have peeled the skin off the inside of Tom's pink mouth. So she'd start cooking it all together; her husband's small chicken legs and thighs with Tom's skinless breasts in one big pot, until Tom's could be rescued and packed in green and orange Tupperware and the rest could be added to, to complete her second order. She didn't even need to dirty two pans.

Vicky's elder son used to sit in the white plastic chair she had brought in from the garden, watching her and getting a feel for getting it right. Learning never to measure, it wouldn't turn out properly, she always insisted. It was all in the eye, the nose and wrist action: tipping powders that had been painstakingly roasted and ground and stored in glass jars that used to hold pasta sauces and mayonnaise; learning not to trust the labels and knowing instead from a shade in colour or coarseness in texture that the paprika was in fact something much hotter.

His favourite recipe was a traditional one, *alla-thel-dhala*, with fried potatoes, onions and garlic, a little crushed chilli, mustard seeds and dried Maldive fish, when that luxury could be procured. Good hot, but better cold, when everyone was asleep and something entertaining came on TV. Usually it was just a repeat of *Cheers*, but if he was lucky he got one he hadn't seen before, and then it was a good night in – with a couple of glasses of wine, and then the last bottle of beer from the fridge. But sometimes Vicky would come down, hearing the noise and join him on the couch, peering over his shoulder as he scoffed to see whether he'd done a good job. Then things could get awkward as Vicky's son turned to his favourites, after dark, on Channel 4. So, after a few minutes she'd be up and in bed again, and he could get on with nibbling on snacks and watching Antoine talk about Lolo's chest.

By herself now, Vicky thought she'd be a little less squeamish about things like that, she could easily have handled a little coarse behaviour. After all, if it proved to be too much she still had a sword to make sure it stopped in good time to protect her modesty. They'd be no need to run up to her room anymore. She knew that her eyes, even though they were now rooted into the head of the girl she had been, had seen enough for her to take a lot to shock.

But Vicky had been a good Catholic girl, and everyone knows there's a lot more out there these days, without Irish nuns to protect and persecute, and the sanctity of a marriage with the blessing of a devout father. Men with a fetish for women's underwear, and women with a passion for rubber and straps. And then the Internet. So much for her to see back there and something for everyone else. But Vicky was so far along in her journey now. She hoped there would be much more to take in when she finally arrived.

Chapter Six

Vicky's last holiday had been to Israel. Not beaches and water sports, but climbing hills, panting hard and clutching prayer cards, keeping her head bowed low – exactly the trip she had been after having studied the brochure, now that she was too old to be let loose dancing.

She had gone with her husband and two of their friends: a doctor who liked to drink with Vicky's husband and talk about the cricket, and his wife who rose early in the morning, an hour before the others, to pray for the day ahead. And she didn't drink, so could get things organised and look after the money, making sure the other three didn't bother the rest too much. There were not too many chances of that on pilgrimage, but Vicky had it mastered, with a little mini bar of a handbag she carried wherever she went, dispensing drinks to the needy when she thought the tour guide wasn't looking.

Vicky was glad of the experience. The path was getting steep now, after miles of flat, and for once she was glad Rex took it slowly. As she huffed and puffed and shouted at him for not picking his feet up she was grateful that she could appear fit and hearty at his expense. She was acting like one of the old nuns who took the girls at her daughter's old school for a run every week – joining them for the beginning of each lap outside the gates and hollering hard for them to get a move on, but dropping back before they turned the corner, leaving the sixth-formers to look after the youngest as they crossed the road and made their way to the beach front, strewn with Coke cans and used condoms.

None of that here, but Vicky couldn't believe that just a few miles back she was running ahead and back like a marathon runner in training, with a partner who should have got the Great North Run under his belt first. Biting off more than she could chew herself, she almost thought about going back. But more than half way up? She knew that would be stupid – she'd have to get over it some time soon, and better now than later, she thought.

But there's nothing wrong with taking a break. She wanted to be back in front of the fire, or sitting at the table with all that food. She wondered whether it would still be warm. But what a silly thought, there would be more of the same and a few better things still to be had just round the bend. Shuffling her feet a little quicker – a forward moon walk, not taking the balls of her feet off the ground – she peered around the next tree and saw exactly what she wanted: a picnic spread on the ground on a red-checked gingham cloth, with hot coffee – she couldn't believe it – and cold juice, orange and apple. She knew little girls shouldn't have caffeine, but the exhaustion of climbing up weighed her body down and she knew she could do with some hyperactivity; especially when she needed to make her own entertainment, with Rex still not speaking.

What a useless pet he had turned out to be. Before she could sit, she had to slip her sword off – over her head and gently to the ground off the round of her right shoulder blade. Then her breastplate and the smooth long hollows and half spheres of her thigh pieces and knee guards – all tied with black ribbon and fastened with a perfect bow. Her eldest son had once told Vicky those leg guards were called greaves. Funny books he read, she couldn't remember how it had come up in conversation. She hoped she could get the bows right when she put them back on, the look was important as their function seemed redundant now. It didn't matter that it took her all that time to get ready to feast either – it looked as if Rex would be a while, shifting his weight from side to side and then down onto the ground. She hoped she'd be able to get him up again once he was finished.

The coffee was hot and the juice so cold it made

Vicky's teeth tingle, so she took a sip from each in turn, not caring that anyone would think it odd. After all, who was going to comment, not Rex – even if he could speak, he really wasn't in a position to comment on other people's table manners.

But her mind couldn't focus on that right now. She was starting to worry about her children. They were taking turns to pull on her left hand and she could feel it. It had made climbing up that bit harder, she liked to think, with strong, young hands pulling her back. Even now with the coffee and juice in her two hands she was afraid she might spill one, and changed them round so the coffee was in her right. No harm done if she did spill with the left then. Maybe she'd give a quick look back later on and a nod and a smile, like they did in films, so they could see it was right, stand back and let her get on with it. But even that might be too much of a distraction. She'd have to wait and see.

She had been sneaking a look every now and again, sometimes when no one was there. What a waste of time that had been. They hadn't a clue what an effort it was for her, as she got further away and held in the landscape unfolding in front of her. And if anything she was honest, at least to herself. She couldn't pretend she wasn't ready, excited to see what it was all about and so tired now that she needed to get somewhere, have a sit down and take it in, bit by bit for all eternity, without the possibility of ever getting bored. What a thought – making her see she might not be quite ready for it to fit into her small head. Her eyes would need to see a bit more before taking in the prize waiting for her at the end. It would just be a waste otherwise, like getting a dog a Gucci collar for Christmas. At least she hadn't bothered with that nonsense for Rex.

Vicky's picnic was a splendid affair. Rex didn't look impressed and barely touched his sandwiches. It didn't help that he needed feeding, and with all this at her fingertips, she wasn't always good at putting down her own to lift his to a slimy mouth and place it on his grey, mottled tongue. It was enough for anyone to be put off their food, and while there was a mountain of it Vicky wanted to make sure she was full. She remembered the training instructions she had seen on numerous planes, on laminated cards and small screens embedded into the seat in front, to make sure you fit your own mask before fitting a child's. It wouldn't make much sense if she worried about Rex first and passed out with hunger.

Vicky hadn't thought properly why he had come along with her. He looked just like the kind of old elephant her father used in the forests to knock over the trees, perpetually looking for one of their graveyards to get away from all the hard work. But it puzzled her. He could quite easily have stayed on the flat of the meadow doing nothing. Why make the effort just to lay down and die? It got her mind to thinking. If he thought the effort was worth making, then there must be something at the end worth making it for. But then again he could just be scared of her and was following now to avoid any confrontation. People could sometimes be a little afraid of her, Vicky had found, for no good reason at all, but it did get things done. She wasn't too sure which she preferred: the idea of scaring an animal the size of a bus, or the idea of what he might be after.

All her favourites were laid out in front of her, so she didn't think about it for too long. Fat white baps dusted with flour and filled with thick slices of pink ham and a thin spread of eye-watering mustard, all of it held together with very good butter; glazed rolls with sliced beef and onions folded into themselves before rising beautifully in the oven; and crumbly brown bread stuck together in triangles with more mayonnaise than tuna flakes. God, she could eat when she was hungry, filling her mouth with glee. Her appetite was certainly renewed after miles of walking and floating lazily downstream from the cottage.

Back in the hospital her family were doing the same, her son having left her alone for a few minutes to join the others. Helen was there – his mother's old friend – accompanied by her mother and son, and her neighbour who had driven them all the way from North

Wales, arriving late after a couple of whirls round the M25. The weather was perfect for sitting in the small patio between the hospital and canteen, filled with dark-green metal garden chairs and tables. But like the back entrance the ground was covered with fag ends and some had been stubbed out on the table and pushed between the gaps in the metal work, sticking halfway through and held fast. Foil drinks cartons too from the vending machine, on seats with crisp packets and coffee cups, half empty with the tubular rims unpicked and chewed. Vicky's eldest couldn't remember the last time he had had one of those lunch box cartons of squash. He used to love freezing the lemon ones to cut them open before they froze solid, to eat with a spoon, because he didn't have one of those machines to make home-made Slush Puppies. They had sold them at Argos and weren't expensive, he couldn't figure out why he hadn't ever got one. It wasn't like he had asked for one at Christmas and got socks and a satsuma instead. It must have slipped his mind to ask with the winter weather. It always snowed on his birthday too.

Helen's mother didn't let his mind wander. She would have been a good one to have around all the time. She wore four-inch stilettos, usually patent leather in red or black, and kept her hair curled tight with a weekly visit to Raymond, who had moved his salon from

Knightsbridge in the early '60s, thinking then that he would like the bracing air of North Wales. Looking exactly the same as Vicky's children remembered from their last visit over ten years ago, keeping the image she liked into her sixties. She might have hit seventy in fact, but it would have been rude to ask, and she certainly didn't care, so what was the point in knowing? Vicky's husband and daughter were not around. But no one thought to ask where they were. So six of them sat about the table in the centre, taking it in turns to deal cigarettes like cards. It was the first time Vicky's boys had seen that. It must have made keeping track of the rounds at the pub that much harder, with the croupier's responsibility working clockwise as the obligation to buy drinks moved the other way round. The thing was it fixed the pace, and because the circle had two new-comers there was no order to it, so as soon as someone wanted to light up again the rest got theirs accordingly, even when they had just finished their last. That worked with pints but not so well here, and they got through forty between them by the time Vicky's husband returned with his daughter, obvious now where they'd been with the evidence of what they were carrying from the shops, a better collection of crisps and chocolate, having exhausted what was on offer here. They had to stop now. Everyone knew Vicky's husband shouldn't really smoke with his bad heart, and it would be hard for him to sit with them and not join in.

Helen had grown her hair long again – fine chestnut strands pulled back hard and falling in a straight line down her back, almost to her waist, much like the way she used to wear it when she had first met Raj. She had started losing the strength in her arms, and this style was the easiest except in the mornings – the repeated action training her shoulders to carry her arms up high and held still for the thirty seconds it took to get it all in place and bound together. Even sitting there you could tell it was difficult for her to pull up a chair, carry the potted plant she had brought for Vicky and smoke at the same time. But her years of balancing other people's children on her hips whilst stirring a big pan of spaghetti had made her perfectly coordinated. Even now, her hips and legs were trained and stronger, to make up for her other less useful limbs.

She was there to change the atmosphere, ease it with old stories and make them laugh with a few new ones. She was doing a fine job too. With her mother warming up the audience and her neighbour John perfect for her to taunt and tease when things got a little quiet. He followed her round like a cumbersome dog, especially after he had lost his own and spent his savings on a very nice service and burial at the pet cemetery just outside Llandudno. Every other day he went and laid flowers and tidied up the plot, coming back to Helen's for a quick cup of tea and a long

laboured stream of insults said with a smile and a wink.
Twenty years ago she could have played this game
with anyone she wanted to at The Black Lion; The
Cow even, if she had stayed to see that scrubbed up
and the dining room open upstairs. But not now – she
had made up her mind to go back and it was too late
to reconsider. She couldn't possibly afford W2 anymore.
Whilst Raj, her ex-husband, had sent his new little
one to a very good boarding school in Hertfordshire,
Helen's son was dodging a screwdriver and a gang of
four fourteen-year-olds. He never had been one to
run fast but you wouldn't really have expected anyone
to get away without a mark, however good they had
been getting off the blocks. He showed them the scars.
Only Vicky had seen these already when she had gone
to see him in hospital, bringing back photos for them
all to see: his pale brown face looking bloated with
purple clots and held together with thick black cord
in a messy running stitch. But none of them had seen
his body before – it would have been a bit much for
Vicky to lift up his gown and make her own record.
But now, in front of three nurses and one doctor on
their break, he lifted up his shirt and traced out the
lines with the flat of the nail of his index finger, carefully – almost like the tip was sharp enough to break
the skin again and reopen the wounds. One of the
nurses came over and said hello to Vicky's eldest son.
The prettiest showing him a little special attention:

Maria, with loose curls of light blonde and mousy brown hair and a soft Sydney accent. Not that he would have picked it out that precisely before she had told him.

Helen pretended not to be pleased, shooing her off to embarrass both of them. It wasn't as if she had been flirting – he didn't think – but Helen didn't like the look of her. She seemed too highly strung and too well made-up for a nurse or either of Vicky's sons. What would she think of all the London girls Vicky's eldest spent each weekend with, tall and blonde, all good Godolphin girls?

The sun had a small opening between the buildings to get through. And for the time they sat there it was warm and bright. Vicky's eldest couldn't help but think he was misremembering it when he looked back at the scene in his mind, but he thought not – it surely would have been a lot greyer if that had been the case. There was the company to think about too; a proper reunion that went very well. No long silences so they sat for hours and talked, with Helen falling into a role immediately, jumping up to get coffees and sandwiches for everyone as if she were still looking after little ones clinging to her skirt.

Vicky's family had begun to wonder where they'd all be staying, her daughter embarrassed thinking about the state of the bathroom. She should have cleaned it the last time she visited, she thought, mended the cracked toilet seat that had broken years before, scraped the dirt from the old grouting that framed the sink. And then there were the bedrooms. Vicky had been on the couch for weeks feeling unwell and her room was a bigger mess than usual with her husband in the middle of tidying up the day she was brought in; things were all over the place, the process of tidying always making more mess first. Chaos theory in the comfort of their own home. And it hadn't felt right to go home each night and do a little more. It would have meant throwing away some of her things without her there to complain that she had kept it all for so many years for a reason. Where were they going to sleep? Vicky's family really started to worry about the arrangements, thinking where they could get spare blankets and pillows from and, in her daughter's mind, whether they'd match and look OK.

Vicky found the whole thing funny, especially when they were stationed back around the bed, paying so little attention to her and more to playing host to the guests they didn't realise she was sneaking a peek. How serious they looked. Like something awful had happened, or they had been asked to organise a wedding in three short days. They'd certainly have their hands full next week.

Helen didn't like seeing Vicky like that, but her son wanted to spend hours sitting by his godmother, talking now and again when he thought no one was listening about his two-year-old son and baby daughter, both of whom would love to see their Aunty Vicky on her next visit. Especially his boy, who would receive a small red metal bus his father had got from one of the tourist shops near the museum and blessed with Vicky's right hand, now wrapped in the scapular the nurses had had to remove from about her neck to rearrange her tubes. A present from his godmother's own hand and only to be played with on special occasions, he would tell the boy, like a dinky toy, only good to sell on if no one can tell it has ever served its purpose. Vicky wondered whether the boy would place as much importance in the small thing as his father did. But she had been surrounded by more spoilt children, who got so much they were bored before they had finished unwrapping it all. Maybe the move out to a small Welsh town on the coast hadn't been a bad idea after all.

The group had found a new place to convene, outside the ward doors, where the original troupe had sat themselves down, expecting a much shorter wait than this. The aunts kept coming and going. Not staying for too long, and rarely bringing their husbands now. They kept the shifts up and missed each other each day, with the Welsh set coming and going with Vicky's husband and children. But the first night they didn't even stay with them, preferring instead to sleep in the car, taking turns on the back seat, with the exception of Helen's son, who was young enough to go without for one night. And the next night they were off having spent a week's salary on flowers, coffee and parking, with sore necks from sleeping sitting up, and dry mouths from all that talking.

Helen said she'd be back when she was needed, with the others as well if more troops were required. But for now, Vicky's eldest sat at home at night and watched the tape of his parents' last trip to Wales to visit her. The year Vicky had bought her husband a second-hand video recorder to play with after years of him wanting one. Everything could now be recorded for times like this, this one showing Vicky slightly slumped over on Helen's shoulder with a glass in her hand at 3 in the afternoon. At least he thought it must have been 3, judging by the sun coming in through the window, and no clock in the frame to document it exactly. She kept not wanting to look into the lens, like a superstitious tribeswoman, or shy adolescent, even though the others were impressed, acting up for the cameraman and making the whole thing a lot funnier than it should have been. And Vicky kept her eyes fixed on Helen, like a small child looking up to an older, worldlier friend. A neighbour's daughter who did everything first and very well, and who liked the attention for the short time it lasted. But Vicky was fifty-five then and Helen couldn't have been more than forty-four. And if the stories were to be believed Vicky had never needed anyone to look to for a lead. In fact she had always been more impressive than this, cruel and funny, making Helen cry early on in their friendship by pretending she had caught her pinching her eldest as he cried in the kitchen of Vicky's small flat in Ladbroke Grove. And Helen didn't think it funny and thought she was being serious and got upset, too young to know Vicky was kidding. Helen seemed to have more authority these days, and Vicky was glad to be in waiting; if only because Helen was a good and beneficent one, strong and resilient too with the air of a good leader.

The video seemed pathetic after a while but Vicky's eldest kept on watching. Helen trying to get Vicky to look at her husband and tell him she loved him. Vicky wasn't having any of it, pushing Helen's flat palm back with the flesh of her right cheek to look at what she wanted to – a grinning white moon of a face, to tell her where her affection lay that afternoon. Vicky's friends had become very important to her as she got older, and she was good at keeping hold of them, through argument, persuasion, and lots of soft loans from people who couldn't afford it, but were sure they were going to help her get through to the end of the month. Her children wondered how she did it, hoping that was one thing they had picked up. Through the genes or with a thousand object lessons, conversations and body language to make the world love you when they know they should know better. Watching the tape you'd never imagine the two women hadn't seen each other for over three years. Vicky's eldest wondered whether that was why so many of his friends had been coming to visit, paying their respects and caring how he was doing. He felt very lucky indeed for a very single young man, much better than weekly dates with girls his friends said he'd love, and yet the conversation still didn't flow.

All the films would come out later, even ones he hadn't seen before. The best was a copy of an old ciné of Vicky on a beach when she couldn't have been older than twenty-eight but must have been. He couldn't think who would have taken it otherwise. It was always his father's job to do that kind of thing and they wouldn't have met each other yet. Either it was someone else behind the lens or she had very good skin.

She was tall and willowy, wearing a loose yellow summer dress blowing in the wind, with thick hair, just long enough to get in the way and too short to stay held back behind her ears, and yet she repeatedly tried. Beautiful seeing her like that, like he wanted to remember her. So much better to see her in something fitting of a memory, however twisted to suit it was. Imagine if his mother had been ugly or boring, stupid even. It wouldn't have made for all these descriptions.

He had seen all the other ones before, but it had been so long they were still worth the watch. Most of them repeated early family holidays, after he was about seven the projector had broken and couldn't be fixed, so ten years went by with albums of photos instead with nothing moving and no sound, until his father's new toy – a good few years after the last big family excursion to Italy. It was the time Vicky's daughter got drunk for the first time – in order to provide some entertainment for her brothers – and threw up over the side of a newly renovated Trevi Fountain. Thank goodness that wasn't captured for posterity, and that she was too drunk to remember what the irate Romans were shouting. A good thing too that she didn't understand Italian, when fragments came back to her in the morning to be pieced together, meaning nothing without the aid of a good dictionary.

The ones when Vicky's eldest was small were old enough to be grainy, making him feel much older than twenty-five. They even skipped now and again where the projector had stopped and started, the spool winding on unpredictably as the VHS copy was being made. In one, he and his brother were pushing their sister through the rain – still bright, but no sign of a rainbow – in a pushchair in the shape of dolphin. It must have been at Sea World, he doubted anywhere else would have rented out rubberised Flippers on wheels. They made figures of eight on the concrete – it looked like a car park, with no cars about – the water parting and staying like that to keep the fat figure whole until a new one was marked out. And then a sudden stop and the small girl's arms flying back, exaggerated and dramatic. Performing for the camera, without a sense of how over-done it was, the toddlers playing slapstick as the rain came down silently. There was music too with some of them. It made the one on the beach seem timeless, with just the whistling of the wind and the click, click, clicking of the film winding on. In actuality it was probably just the video threatening to chew the tape, he must get a new one, Vicky's eldest thought. The others had pieces that marked them out perfectly, the tunes a few years old even for the picture, their father not young enough then to keep up with the charts. So, it was the theme from the BBC coverage of the first Sri Lankan test tour from 1982, which had got a lot of play then, and then again afterwards at home when Vicky's husband bought the single from John Menzies on the high street. The children's uncle even had the commemorative plate. They must have won, and he must have bought that song too to remember the occasion. It didn't matter as much, as it had been years since Vicky's children had heard it play with all the vinyl packed away into boxes. Records by all sorts, even Lionel Ritchie with the video alive in Vicky's eldest's head, of him bursting into song with a receiver in his hand, or actually face-to-face with a beautiful blind girl and a clay head that looked nothing like him. And as ridiculous as the video was it reminded Vicky's eldest of life at ten, but that was stupid, because his thinking was all wrong. He couldn't have been more than seven at the time and even if he could remember the song from then (he had forced his father to start buying him singles from the age of six, he liked to think Blondie, but more often than not Bucks Fizz) it certainly wouldn't have drawn such clear images in his mind from his life back then. His memory was playing tricks, working proleptically as it did, fluid but comfortable in the confusion. A good word from a book he had read at college when he studied the *Faerie Queen* with Professor Anderson. But then again, there was always a chance just the sounds were enough to be tied to something else, however tangential the connection was. No one ever said words in songs actually meant anything. Not many people paid close attention to them at all – even the ones who could sing along perfectly without needing the inside sleeve to help them along.

Enough about the music, it wasn't what gripped any of them anyway. The line of a face and sloping teeth in huge smiles sat on small faces were much more the thing.

Vicky's meal could have done with a little music. The whole affair had gone on so long, it seemed like it was unwinding in slow motion, with every second frame missing like an animation wheel to be played on a turntable and made by a five-year-old thanks to the make-and-mend slot on *Blue Peter*. With the food not stopping but the plates and jugs still full, it could have been one, with the pure repetition of action: lifting a cup, sipping and down, up and down, and a reach over to take another sandwich. And with the focus off the plate, no one would have noticed that the same sandwich was back and ready for her hand. This could go on forever. But as soon as Vicky was full she was going to get up and get going. No point wasting precious time because of greed. She wondered what her eldest would do in her place. He wouldn't quit now, give it up and get up off the ground, with such a spread tempting him to stay.

The canteen had started offering a better selection. The family had figured out how to get the best stuff, waiting till the end of serving hours when the staff came in and the menu changed. It wasn't like they didn't have enough to go around, and they were all happy paying the money for it too. After a couple of days some of the staff recognised them and didn't think to remind them when the visitors' hours were. Then there were the other restaurants to explore. But it never seemed like a good idea unless they were by themselves with friends over for the afternoon. A family outing would have gone too well, with the chance to sit outside, enjoy the sun and talk. They never usually managed to book ahead for the lunchtime rush on Sundays, or get up and out, ready in time on the few occasions they did.

Vicky's eldest had gone to another one of the pubs across the square, this time face-to-face with the red bricks, and had left his brother with his sister and a few of her in-laws who were making their first visit. It was all sounding serious, they thought. Vicky's eldest was meeting a friend who had come by to see Vicky after selling anti-inflammatories downstairs to some of the doctors. And it would have been embarrassing to stay and watch him talk to her, with such a crowd already there, so many unfamiliar faces. So it was the pub, a couple of pints, some conversation and a few remarks that Vicky's eldest knew were inappropriate and sounded flippant before he even spoke them out loud. But things like that were meant to happen, so people could look at him strangely, tilting their heads and speaking softly as they looked like they understood, or loudly in an effort to talk over it. And that's what he was doing himself, hearing the words getting louder as he drank and the people on the next table looked over, staring as they tilted their heads and forced a smile at him too.

Chapter Seven

When Vicky's husband was eighteen he had been chased out of the field next door by an angry neighbour with a gun, for climbing up a tree and stealing fruit with his friends. Telling the story now he couldn't remember what kind of fruit it was, the gap in his memory making him realise the trouble hadn't been worth it after all. His children looked at him strangely as he thought and tried to remember the details, finding it impossible to imagine a night out like that.

Vicky's eldest had always liked planning the nights he was going to have when he was old enough to get served, standing by the bar, secure and at ease in the silence of other people's conversations going on around him. Thinking about all the things he wasn't supposed to be thinking about yet, at his age, and who he might get a chance to do all that with. And when the time came he chose the blondes with long and soft hair, which didn't register with him until he was twenty, and hadn't done so well impressing Emily and Celia at the college bar, or thought it strange that he never fancied Nita, who served behind it, like most of his friends. But that was another story. It could be quite interesting though, even make for another chapter. But he supposed everyone chased after the ones who ran away.

All his cousins had boyfriends and girlfriends from school and the local club – the pink, plastic paradise eight miles away in Watford where the action happened outside: the fights out front after the music had stopped and liaisons out back when the music was loud enough for the boys to suggest to the girls they continue their conversations where it was quiet and dark. And a disorderly line would form each weekend, the boys standing shy but determined, with their left hands awkwardly around a hip to hold them close with the right exploring until it was slapped off. Vicky's nephews had enjoyed moments like that with Karen and Nicki from the year below them at school. All of them looked like extras from *Grange Hill*, shot not far away, in the car park at Debenhams and the local leisure centre when the script called for the kids to come out and play, smoke and get into trouble, when they should have been swimming. Karen's mother wouldn't have liked the association; Nicki's parents wouldn't have been as bothered. But she got pregnant, had the baby and quickly moved on to a flat off Camden Road and a new boyfriend who didn't live with his parents.

All of the extended family were a little more cautious about coupling their children off to the locals after that, having first thought it might be the key to settling further into the new life. None of them went back very much anyway, and they didn't talk about going *home* when they did – not after thirty years, and all the slight changes in their voices that would sound odd, a conscious change. And then the fear that people would think their move a dismissive betrayal; they had left and not wanted to return for good, had made the decision and now had to stick to it, unless they wanted to go back to dead friends and houses that had fallen down on roads that had been renamed.

One of Vicky's in-laws had started to support England in the test matches when they weren't playing Sri Lanka, though it wasn't difficult for him to choose when they did. Still, not the thing for a good Asian man to do; his Indian neighbours would think he had defected, appropriating a new sense of pride, and presuming that that was OK. But in his mind it was all about religion – not that he ever practised – and he didn't realise it was a bad idea to blame religion for differences and similarities like that. It was like talking politics over dinner; things are sure to get heated. But he did only speak English, and had been taught as a little one to pray to a God who, although not in the exact image of the one he found when he got to North London, was a much closer cousin than Ganesh.

And the network of Vicky's family did like the idea of their importance to the rising and sprawling middle classes; making them feel proud when they got it right, like they had picked up the message sent to them over thousands of miles and carried it back, a little purer.

The families had all settled in quite quickly though, and thankfully they managed to steer clear of too much thinking like that. Vicky's husband hadn't got the first job he applied for but wouldn't let it bother him, not even after seeing the sign in the window the next time he passed on the way to the shops and they were recruiting again, stating clearly that Blacks, Asians and Irish need not apply. It was just a shame he had wasted a stamp and not dropped it round in person to see it wasn't worth responding to the advert. It was only an assistant's job at a tailor's in Paddington anyway, and he was studying to become a business leader, a manager or supervisor, and had no idea how to chalk and cut across the warp of an expensive roll of worsted. He could face having to go back to school in the evenings to put a more practical spin on his ten years of teaching if it was going to get him somewhere, where cream-coloured cartridge paper detailed with italicised script and official stamps meant something. And he certainly couldn't face the secondary modern the wrong side of the Westway that had got him over in the first place, to fill a post no one in London wanted. But that meant the visa had come quickly, he just had to wait to save a little money for the trip.

All these big plans meant that Vicky's husband had to work hard, working a full day as an office junior and then studying at the dining table in the back room of the new house Vicky had managed to get through telling tales. They were tales about the money she had stashed away in Sri Lanka which was being sent over any day now by her father, the diplomat, dressed in a sari for the first time since she had come to London, wearing all her jewellery at once in front of the bank manager to make her story very convincing. In fact they had drawn up a list of twenty people they knew – which had to include a woman she met every day on the platform on the way to work as they hadn't been there long – borrowing five pounds from each to put down a deposit. And while they paid them all back in turn they ate lentils and rice, and on Saturdays she curried chicken wings – a good deal at 15p for a full polystyrene tray at the end of the day, on her way back from the office. She didn't like to think why they were more expensive in the morning.

Vicky's children couldn't remember things like that. By the time they were old enough to remember anything clearly their father had qualified near the top of his class years before, and had been working a good long while, taking out three credit cards and two home improvement loans to build a larger kitchen and an extra bedroom above that. None of them could imagine waiting for meat in the shops to go grey and shiny

– like petrol caught in expansive shallow puddles – before they bought it, a necessary bargain. And that had driven Vicky and her husband to fight, out of frustration. Even her skilled hands couldn't make a delicious meal out of such poor ingredients, and her husband, out of pride, would shout that she should know better and pay the extra even if they couldn't afford it when one meal had them laid up in bed for three days. But people change, softening over the years like overripe bananas, with the luxury of a little money to make firm bodies fleshy with hard-earned new indulgence. And every good grocer knows that bananas can help the rest along in a tightly packed fruit bowl. Even the stall on the high street sold their stock off hooks, perched in small clumps, held away like children who might be a bad influence.

Vicky's fruit was just perfect, she thought. And to think that it still wasn't something that usually bothered her – the black spots just making her eat faster, with a sense of urgency.

Vicky's husband was keen on extra-curricular activities for his children, filling each evening with long drives to take them to learn things he had no idea about. There was ballet for his little girl, football for his middle boy and the violin for his eldest; chosen on a whim after seeing a young man on TV fiddling away with transfixing dexterity to a large and well-dressed audience. But he just wouldn't practise – although he did show a little promise at the Christmas recital one year after the best in his group changed seats to sit next to him to mask the noise he was making – and so he decided to try something else.

The piano was much more his thing, the idea of striking a key and getting a perfectly pitched note – assuming it wasn't at the lower end of the keyboard two days after it had been tuned – a lot easier to understand. Now it was only rhythm to master, getting used to marking out time with one hand tapping his left leg, the other his right, none of it really giving any idea of how to get duplets and triplets working together like they did in *Bohemian Rhapsody*, even though his teacher thought it might help. It must have seemed easy money those two weeks, though very boring for him. But in the end Vicky's eldest got it, and there was nothing like being able to bang out a recycled number one for his music class at school when they were trying to get to grips with simplified versions of theme tunes from TV soaps. The school had chosen to hire a pretty twenty-four-year-old cellist as their music teacher, and none of the boys were interested in learning that, though they paid close attention to her as she introduced them to concertos that sounded odd without an orchestra but still had them mesmerised. Now if she had only been able to play so well on his three-quarter-size Stentor violin Vicky's eldest might have made a go of it.

His piano playing made him popular amongst a few of the others, especially the other secret musicians who had been forced from seven to practise hard, but would never be allowed to learn anything that wasn't going to get them a certificate. Even a few of the others showed him attention as they tried to learn what he knew quickly to show off to girlfriends but got bored and opted for carving their initials on the sweeping side of the grand black Bechstein borrowed from the church next door (indefinitely, after one of the legs came loose and it was clearly not going back easily).

Vicky's eldest liked to think he could sing too, based principally on his selection at seven, along with one other girl, to sing two solo verses of a hymn at the beginning of the year's First Holy Communion Mass. They sang the last together with the class, both of them trying to get their voices heard over the others, even if that meant missing the beat just a little, or refusing to finish the last note after the piano had stopped. It wasn't like it had particularly gone to his head or his parents'; Nina's had moved the family seven miles into town to be closer to the stage school she started at the following year. After three episodes in *Johnny Briggs* (playing one of the kids in his class who said very little, and never being scripted into the cellar scenes, where all the interesting things happened), she did the rounds at musical auditions, before deciding to do the circuit in West End bars in front of disinterested audiences where she had heard there was still plenty of work. He wondered if she was still singing. He certainly wasn't, except very softly in his bedroom, trying to emulate a variety of singer-songwriters. Ridiculous for a twice-broken voice – and he had to try and change the pronouns round every line so it would make sense. Not that anyone was listening.

The first time Vicky's eldest's voice broke it was in the middle of rehearsals for another musical at school, although luckily this was his first and he was only singing with the chorus. It wasn't too bad at all though, and for nearly six months he could sing all four parts of the William Byrd piece Miss McKeever got a few select boys to sing when the bishop came to say Mass for the governors and a small number of parents who wanted to show their support. But then in Wales, on a science field trip at the end of Easter term, it happened for good, in front of a small audience – three friends, who had collectively been given the granny flat four flights up and one building across from the '50s dormitory the other boys had to stay in. They had high ceilings and large windows overlooking the hills they spent cold mornings on collecting soil samples and learning how to use a very basic theodolite. Real ones cost nearly £5000, they were told, even the ones they had should be handled with care. There was even a bathroom of their own to share and a few mice that had been attracted to the food and lager they had smuggled along with them and hidden under one of the wardrobes. And they had been given the space because they were the mature and reliable ones. To think they had caused an infestation worthy of calling out two men in an old Vauxhall van, all the way from Abergavenny to the tiny outpost nestled in the green.

It wouldn't have been so embarrassing if Vicky's eldest hadn't been singing along to some Joni Mitchell. They had each brought a few tapes along with them and this was one of his choices and he sang along with the words to make sure they got them, and could see why he liked it all so much and hadn't brought something more modern with him. And right in the middle of *For The Roses* – strange for a sixteen-year-old boy to be singing from that album to his male friends – it happened; shattered completely a good two years after most of the rest (he should have been grateful for the extra few miles) and in the company of others. Vicky's eldest never sang in public again. Trying just the once the following year, and realising he could only muster an octave and a half comfortably.

Five years beforehand he had made it to the Albert Hall to sing with two hundred other eleven-year-olds – a vast gathering of school choirs from across North London who had been forced to whittle down their numbers and provide only ten of their best. Not difficult in their case, as they only had thirteen, two were sick, and Geraldine didn't like singing in front of a large audience. They were given a name for the day: The North London Regional Schools' Choir. Very official, with a capital stamp that would have made a good acronym if there had been more vowels to plump it out. And the whole point of one of those was to make it easier to say as they got bigger and better, starting a tour maybe, and making a constant reference would have been a mouthful. But that was their only outing, and Vicky's eldest was a bit too old for it when they re-formed for another one-off eight years later.

Vicky's eldest liked getting involved in things like that to keep him away from anything too physically strenuous, his brother on the other hand loved football and rugby and his sister could wield a hockey stick with enough conviction to part the opposition like the Red Sea. He did nearly make it into the swimming team though, having got good at pushing himself off fast and letting the momentum behind his weight keep him going. It worked for mile-long efforts better than the short relays, with the others having to work too hard at keeping afloat for that long without the buoyancy of a full belly. This, however, was a singular attempt at going for the medals. It might have actually been just a certificate though, he couldn't remember. And when it counted he missed the schools' championships as his asthma kicked in, and he had to go to hospital for the week. As soon as the attack started it stopped, like a small precursory heart spasm with no real sign of it left so things can go back to normal, as long as you take heed and are careful. A pity, he thought at the time, he had liked the attention in the ward – with aunts coming by and slipping him packets of crisps, and the teacher in the small classroom (for the ones who'd be in for months) thinking he was very bright indeed; sitting him down the second day he came in and timing him complete block puzzles and word and number games. As the other three in the class fought over the one computer, with a green and black screen, to play *Martello Tower*.

It was different at school. The teachers had to deal with a class of thirty and knew they had a reliable one in him and a few of the others. Jamie still couldn't read properly, and long division was going to take forever. They certainly didn't have the time to keep telling him how well he was doing and where they thought he'd end up after another ten years of hard work. Now that would have been useful. He hadn't a clue what he'd end up doing, not realising that the others didn't either, and the few who did were still thinking of flying planes and playing football. The girls wanted to be on *Top of the Pops*, dancing and fawning behind the man with the mike.

Vicky had finally finished her very long meal, sure that it would be enough to get her there without another break. And surprisingly Rex was quick off the mark, jumping up just as she finished the last mouthful. Thank goodness for that, she thought. She couldn't deal with his inertia on a full stomach, when she had her own to think about.

In the distance she could hear hooves hitting the ground hard, the sound of thousands of feet moving together and fast in one direction. She wanted to see which way they were heading and get a clue for herself, hoping the herd wasn't being chased by something that would like the taste of a well-fed small girl. Over the hedge to her right she knew she'd catch sight of them soon, the sound getting louder without a visual trigger, like a tube approaching from round the bend – announcing its arrival more accurately than a dot matrix countdown. Getting impatient, thinking they should be here already, she peered over the trimmed green leaves, on tiptoes so only the top of her head would show. And the sight was breath-taking: a pale bay mount a furlong in front, leading a cloud of dust hiding a number so large it would have to remain a mystery. And as it passed she realised it was far too big to be like any horse she had seen, though its proportions looked perfect as far as she could make out, her eyes only able to take in the reach of its four muscled legs this close up. And it raced on past her, fast but in control, and so the fear of a chase left her, as the thousands that followed engulfed her in their cloud as they tried frantically to keep up.

Staggering back, sputtering and coughing, Vicky tripped over herself and landed on the ground. Rex stood still nearby waiting for a decision, which she knew she'd have to make herself, not being able now to see any more which way they had all gone if she wanted to follow too.

Vicky felt freer to get on with it now, left by herself for the first time in her bed, without the nurses fussing over her every hour through the night whilst families and friends slept. Maria was talking about her night out and she wanted to listen in, but she was sitting at the nurses' station with her colleagues by the doors and it was difficult to hear, with a keen audience of older women all too tired to use their nights off like that any more. Her voice moved quickly and the accent didn't help. Vicky was never very good at those, having spent the last ten years barely able to understand her boss, Damian, who claimed to be Swiss. It made her last appraisal almost impossible, save for the figures on the sheet in front of her. No raise and no bonus. She assumed she hadn't done that well, but then again she could have been one of the lucky ones not to get the chop. She didn't know whether to be annoyed or grateful, smiling slightly and saying little as he explained what her new targets should be.

Hearing just the slightest bits of Maria's conversation had got some confusion going. It had been a long while since she had done the things she was over-hearing, what a Friday she had had out with her friends, and Vicky couldn't even remember the name of the pub opposite her office when she had gone there so many times years before. Maybe she should go back and find out. There was no doubting that her newly found youth had swayed her, made her think it was wonderful just to be able to walk briskly and run that she hadn't thought whether she wanted to keep on going. But she had felt it was right, even had a better idea which way to go now. But what if everyone got duped into it just like that? Happy to have the blood flowing and colour in their cheeks, food on demand and endless sunshine. Like a drug, she thought. At least what she always thought it would be like to be on them. Her children hadn't been any good at getting the idea of all that across when she had asked that one time, not realising that wasn't quite the question she should have been asking.

She hoped she would know what to do. She had already started to get quite used to having her energy back, and she remembered not even thinking about the sun when she was a girl. It was only when she got to London and the flat grey skies weighed her down for six months of the year that she remembered how hot it used to get. And then it was too much again. After another few days of this she'd take it all for granted, she knew, just like Rex must have done. There was no other way of explaining his laziness. Just like when napping starts taking up the whole day, and you forget what you're resting in readiness for, or why it's happiness itself to sit in the sun and indulge in an all-you-can-eat buffet by the side of a pool three hundred yards from a glorious white-sand beach. But how long before the indulgence becomes excessive? She remembered herself, sitting in her chair, or lying on the couch and waiting for the day to pass so she could say, finally, time for bed. She would have loved to have had the chance to do that at forty, but it was more than boring now – when the thought of work was going, with an alarm to get you up, because you must, in the morning.

It was starting to feel like that as she walked, not content any more just to keep on going for no reason; wilderness walking in one large oasis, with all the wild horses too fierce to tame. If it was actually so wonderful the children would have played with her and she wouldn't have been left by herself. Even Rex was walking faster now, leaving her a pace behind every time she took two and he took three – for they covered the same ground here with each stride, even though she was the size of one of his feet lying down. How did that work, she thought, getting annoyed that she was getting distracted again, with things that meant nothing. She didn't want him to get away before she knew what she was doing. His speed might mean he knew the way now, and although not one to follow Vicky knew it was stupid to let him get out of her sight. Just in case. But what was the point of keeping up if she wasn't sure, and he still wasn't speaking? So she stood still as he walked and let the lead slip out of her hand.

Vicky felt like a sleep, realising she hadn't had one for ages and that her shuffle wasn't walking off lunch. Things would be clearer then in a funny way, with everything floating about in her head between two places, a jumble she could at least have all in front of her to decipher and sort and make some sense of. Even when she was at home it was how she worked, though obviously not in her sleep. Placing things side by side: a full tumbler claimed after she collected the twelve labels she needed for a whole set, and a new card effigy sent to her by one of her friends in Kent. Only then could she make the call, being able to fall deeply for either when the other wasn't pitching hard enough for her attention. And she felt she hadn't given the rest a fair enough chance at winning her back. She felt like a spoilt child, so busy playing with her favourite present to even realise she had a dozen more scattered about at her feet and she hadn't even thought to make a card herself to return to say thank you, gratefully.

★   ★   ★

Vicky's life was neatly split in three. She saw it now. The beginning, rarely mentioned, seemed so far away it was like someone else's; the middle – made without plan but with her own two hands – whizzed by with work and children, parties and holidays. And when the break came in preparation to start the last part she had tried to get through it quickly, not seeing the point. While she slept the whole thing passed, the sound and sense of it flashing back in whirls like she was drowning, going down the plughole. But the water kept going round – as it does in any bath with the enamel worn thin with her held in the centre with nothing concrete to hold onto – a little always left until suddenly the final glug.

Watching it all like that Vicky saw everything so clearly. Now if only she had seen that in the first place she would have held on a little tighter and enjoyed the best bits more. There wasn't enough dancing, too many mornings on trains and evenings slumped in an armchair watching scripted lives. She paused and looked harder, not able to recognise the padded brown velvet of the old three-piece suite at first. It was only with closer inspection that she saw the snaked back-springs poking out prematurely, so much so it had to be replaced quickly and erased from memory as a bad buy. Lucky she had the controls with her, to pause and replay and good too that she could use them without opening her eyes. She had had a lot more difficulty with the ones at home. One count against going back, those controls. Every little thing would have to be considered. A few at least, to help with the bigger ones.

She opened one eye to see how far Rex had got and was relieved to see he wasn't far off at all. The path was long and wide and still he kept to the right, leaving space for her. That never happened on the Continent. Or on Ekanayake Avenue either, where Vicky had nearly had her first accident, sitting on the back of a bike and holding onto the man in front a little too tightly, her father had thought, as she left the drive, leaving more dust in the air pierced through with the excitement of her laughter. She couldn't see any turnings in the path that lay in front of her now and it stretched on almost forever until it hit a peak miles off, where she assumed the ground levelled off or went down. She had time enough to shut both eyes again and catch up if she wanted to. Rex wasn't going to go out of eyeshot for quite a while. As long as she needed, she knew.

Chapter Eight

1983 had been a big year. Nothing worthy of grand celebrations – no silver anniversaries, eighteenth or twenty-first birthdays, not even a fiftieth. Vicky did, however, throw her husband a big surprise party that year with a cake with a model Kawasaki bike sat on top because her younger boy wanted to keep it to play with. Her husband looked puzzled with the choice, never having been drawn to the open road like that. He was more of a rambler, enjoying long walks when he could get away to see the country, armed with his favourite *Wainwright*, whilst the rest of his family idled at home.

He wasn't pleased with any of it; embarrassed with the attention and calculating the cost of an unwanted gathering with drinks flowing and food piled on plates, sitting on every table in the house, brought down from each of the bedrooms along with stools and chairs to hold the guests as their stomachs swelled. But after a few quick whiskies he was pleased with the fuss, Vicky thought, happier herself to have been the ringmaster than the lady on the white horse.

Vicky Had One Eye Open

The party had been a way to soften her husband to an idea she had had. Vicky had decided it was time for a trip to see her relatives – really just to hold her sister Lucy's hand as she gave birth to her first child. She had moved with her husband to England and back whilst trying for him, thinking a change of scenery would do the trick. And she had looked after Vicky's children in between too, even when Vicky's daughter had had whooping cough and her eldest got chicken pox. What a good mother she'd make, given the chance. But Vicky's husband didn't want to go, didn't have many people to see, having visited his brother and sister three years beforehand already. He thought that California would be much more interesting, with burgers and amusement arcades for the kids and the big national parks and a crashing ocean for him. But Vicky wasn't convinced, wasn't sure what they'd have to keep her amused, and so booked the tickets she wanted on her husband's credit card, packed off the three children and left before the bill came through in the post. He knew they were going of course, and that he was paying, but he didn't want to talk about it until they got back home safely. There would be time for arguments then, with the worry of men with guns, riots and curfews less vivid in his mind.

None of the children could remember exactly how long the trip had been. It did seem like a very long time to them, with family coming and going, some from London too. All of them were waiting eagerly for the baby to arrive, the last of this generation, and a very special treat for some of them who were on the verge of buying toys for their grandchildren. But there was nothing to do for the little ones, it was surprising how well behaved they were, the sun must have kept them tired. They stayed in a large house on the edge of the city, filled with cousins their age to keep them entertained. But the house had lost its grandeur, with a small factory room attached at the rear now and thirty young girls making brushes from coconut husks for their uncle, and a TV with a wire coat hanger – certainly Joan Crawford hadn't visited – sticking out of the back, with terrible reception, showing programmes from the '70s and others they couldn't understand. They got the routine quickly enough to fill the days: rising early to play out in the front yard from breakfast to lunch, playing inside when the sun got too hot, and making their way to the small sweet shop at the end of the road as the sun went down to buy powdery peppermints whilst they waited for the cooks to finish dinner. And like good tourists, they asked for chips with everything, forcing one of the young servants to get on his bike and find potatoes for them when the fried plantain wasn't a good enough substitute. Vicky's children were fussy eaters. She had had to bring two jars of peanut butter for her daughter to smear onto bread whenever she complained about the feast in front of her, feeding it to the small girl as she ate from both of their plates secretly. Making inroads into the steaming plateful in front of her daughter – far too much for a seven-year-old anyway – trying hard not offend her sister and the cook. And no one knew what was in the small glass jars Vicky brought to the table with the labels peeled off, assuming it was a condiment that went well with the fried anchovies.

It was only a matter of time before one of the servants decided to find out for himself, sneaking into their room and taking both to try tentatively with a finger tip at first and then a whole scooping hand, hidden under the slats of a bed so no one would catch him enjoying this new taste sensation. But Vicky did, bending low and pulling up the dirty hem of the muslin mosquito net, thinking she should have them washed the next day. But it was too late – all gone and sitting in a full stomach below a queer, sickened face. She almost thought they'd have to go home before the baby was born. Or leave her daughter to lose a little weight while she threw tantrums in the sun.

The rest of the world was a very long way away. Letters took weeks coming from abroad, and phone lines crackled, connecting town to town, struggling to reach further and forcing the conversations louder. It would have been easier to use two polystyrene cups and a very long, taut piece of string, as the infrastructure of old cables, roads and rail tracks collapsed in the wake of the next generation of independent government. Messages were still sent on foot and by bike, with half the servants kept on and fed for that reason alone – hundreds filling up the dirt paths, passing each other and waving as they ran from house to house to invite the owners over for tea or carrying important letters to grateful recipients, to thank them for dinner and gifts. A teardrop island cut off and happy, left dangling off the coast of the mainland; rich with everything a tourist could want, once the fighting had stopped and they could revamp the colonial mansions with a coat of white paint and build uglier, shiny towers leaning over the side of the south and west coasts.

Vicky's journey with the children hadn't started off well. They were hijacked just outside the airport parking lot by two men with guns who didn't seem to know where they wanted to go. The children's uncle was driving them in his big green American van, with banquette seats in the back. In the darkness and sitting in the back with her three children Vicky hadn't seen the reason why her brother-in-law had stopped dead in the street, assuming it must have been a misplaced traffic light on the half-laid road. She should have known better, but she had spent much time in an ordered suburb where road rules applied. It wasn't until the side door was opened and slid across to reveal the guns, old shaky hands, and then two dark faces hidden in the night air did she think, pushing her youngest under her feet and the bench, knowing her two boys would have been too big to fit down there with her. She had done her best and looked up to heaven innocently. She shuffled to the right and let the two men – both far too short and old to be taken seriously, she thought – sit down before they gave their roundabout instructions to her brother-in-law.

They made him drive to Negumbo, a small fishing town north of the city – in the direction of where they were heading anyway, so no matter really – and through the streets to find a friend of theirs who would be waiting on a corner somewhere. It wouldn't have been that bad but they passed the house they'd be staying at three times as they did the rounds in search of the elusive terrorist who had obviously got himself lost after the sun had gone down. It quickly became ridiculous, making Vicky laugh when she knew she probably shouldn't be doing that in front of men with guns. The van drew to a sudden halt again and the police commissioner jumped in to sit up front. He was on his way home, spotted the van and realised his friend was driving. Surely he wouldn't mind giving him a lift? Just a short way, not too far out of your way, he had said. The men in the back hid their guns under the seat, sandwiching Vicky's daughter between the cold metal and the dented side of the van – a small relief from the heat for her – and were introduced to the commissioner along with Vicky and her two visible children as relatives from England. He looked a little confused. He assumed one of them was Vicky's husband, but what about the other? But he was hungry and wanted to get home, turning back to face the road to direct his old friend to the house he hadn't invited him to since his last promotion. Round the corner the two in the back asked to be let out, still not having found their friend, stupidly mistaking the commissioner's indifference for calm. Calm that must have disguised his plans to get out safely himself only to send some of his men on a chase after them. And after all they weren't actually going anywhere in particular very quickly, and needed to go slow to keep an eye out. So, Vicky and her children – the youngest retrieved from the dirty floor and brushed down – were left to go back the way they had come to arrive at her sister's house with the fluorescent lights burning on the veranda, as the family waited out to see why they had been delayed.

Certainly not the way Vicky wanted the holiday to start. And not a story she was going to share with her husband on their return.

That night Vicky's eldest saw his first snake. Thankfully it was from the comfort of a chair just by the front screen door, but close enough for him. His uncle saw his reaction, hopped out of his chair and down the four steps to the dirt yard. Picking it up confidently he brought its head round to his, looked straight into its eyes as a tongue shot out, almost to kiss him, and laughed. A madman, Vicky's eldest thought. There had been a lot of laughter for a night of hijacking and guns and snakes all far too close up. No wonder the stories managed to travel thousands of miles to London. He wondered about the ones he hadn't heard.

There was a well in the back garden and a stone bath. Vicky thought she'd leave it to the morning to wash the children. Even in this heat, it was better to leave them to sweat than scare them with the wonders of the tropical bush out back, where the lack of lights welcomed in stranger creatures than a yard snake. She knew that bathing after sunset was never a good idea, with all the things that made their way to the bottom of the deep tub, to bite toes and crawl up arms to unsuspecting faces, remaining till the morning when the sun scared them off.

They ate their first meal together, with Vicky's other sisters and long-forgotten second cousins brought over to see their strange-sounding relatives. Vicky's eldest wondered whether he'd go back with an accent like theirs. It would certainly stick out in the playground. Their voices were thick and hard to understand; rising, falling and lilting, with the words turning in on themselves and difficult to distinguish. Vicky's daughter thought it was beautiful, musical almost, and certainly more powerful than the thoughts that fashioned the words. It was like seeing an opera in German, though she was too young to afford all that just yet. The hand gestures got the ideas across and the costumes were fantastic – the old men in orange and blue sarongs and white vests, the old women loosely wrapped in diaphanous cream-coloured saris, layered thick to ensure they remained modest and hid the tyre about their midriff which had taken shape after five children.

The servants made Vicky's children feel very welcome and spoilt. Apart from their clothes it was difficult to tell them apart from the rest. They didn't stand around to attention as they ate, walking in the background instead, keeping silent, as the conversations continued, like more distant relatives awaiting their turn to speak. They lived in a large room behind the kitchen, sleeping on mats communally, even though some were married and had children. Vicky's children got to inspect it all on the tour afterwards. A few had their own homes but stayed over so they could be on call, making families and raising their children as they worked, using the money they were paid to build houses to keep them when they were too old to sleep on mats on the floor. On Sundays they visited their families and went to church, buying food from street vendors outside as a treat to eat as they caught up on the week. And then back to work. Some of the older ones stayed on too though, to continue looking after the children and seeming the perfect grandparent–criminal hybrid, far too familiar with the lifestyle to get on with their own life for the last few years on the outside.

Vicky's eldest boy took a shine to one called Carla, a name his grandfather had given her before he left for London because it was similar to the Sinhala for *black*. And she was dark; a good two shades darker than he was and he wasn't the fairest in the family, with huge white teeth, the front two sticking so far out and at different angles she couldn't close her mouth properly, forcing her to look happy. Her permanent grin got his attention when he arrived, making him think her fun. The look had scared Vicky's younger son and daughter after the excitement of the ride there. Either way, Carla was going to be the perfect companion, when he had worried that his cousins would not want to play. He needn't have, for all his cousins were still young enough, without sticker-collecting and a religious devotion to the *Now* albums, they'd continue playing outside and getting their clothes dirty until they got married. And for some reason drinking had gone out of fashion. No chance of the fifteen-year-olds getting into that kind of mischief or being aggrieved at having to look after a set of small cousins.

Now that was refreshing. All three of Vicky's children had had very different experiences with their cousins in London the few times they were given the unwanted responsibility of looking after three small ones when the childminder was sick. One time they went as far as feigning death in the garden in the middle of a storm – striking so much fear into Vicky's children that they ran to the phone and called their mother on the work number they each had memorised. It was a lot kinder to get them to do their chores and lock them together in one of the bedrooms whilst the elder children invited friends over to drink small sips of malt whisky and Russian vodka from the drinks cabinet. None of them would have minded that too much, particularly Vicky's eldest, who was already developing a worrying fondness for keeping things in order. Even his school books where stacked by size and filed alphabetically when he was old enough to have a sufficient number to make it worth the while.

Back in Sri Lanka, Vicky's eldest had expected more of the same – the kind of treatment he himself handed out when he was lumbered with minding the neighbour's children at fourteen. No blood ties to feel guilty about when he didn't want to watch the video the young boy's mother had left out for him, instead making the four-year-old watch *LA Law* whilst eating takeaway curry rather than the pizza she had left money for.

Even though the cousins in Sri Lanka were happier with the task of keeping him occupied, Vicky's eldest attached himself to Carla from the first night, and she took to him with the kind of affection you'd expect from an old spinster who'd always wanted her own. She was only nineteen, but she knew how to hold a toddler on her hips or a baby in one arm, shifting from left to right when the weight grew too much, to get on with her work. Vicky's eldest could remember being carried like that, and wished he was a little smaller, young enough to get away with not standing on his own two feet.

All the walls were white with red floors that coloured the soles of feet that passed over them, to stain the sheets in bed later. He wondered what they were made of – certainly not tile or lino, something more organic, leaving its mark and being worn thin but never disappearing completely. Vicky's eldest liked to leave his mark too, carving initials and dates where he wasn't supposed to, on the tree in the garden, on the wall by his bed. It was his way of recording important events without the space for a full explanation that a diary would have offered, testing him to remember when he stumbled back upon them. He liked to see how much he could remember and forget, always conscious that lives went by and got misplaced along the way. His father couldn't remember his grandparents' names, where they had lived or what they had done. Not that it mattered, Vicky's eldest supposed, not everyone did things worthy of chronicling. And even if they did, it would have taken too long to read.

Away in a foreign place, he started to leave his mark,

bored when Carla was too busy with work. Along with letters scratched in the white chalk paint he liked using the black rubber soles of his shoes to draw on the floor. Making it seem like an accident, but a strange one at that, as only the edge of a heel gave any precision and it should have looked funny, him skidding along on them with a plan on where to go exactly. Carla gave him his first slap when she finally realised, pulling back from the lines that she had had to polish off to remove another layer still, to see the picture complete. Two firm strokes across his tiny backside and he never did that again, not here at least, and not at home for a while. Not until a few years later and the bathroom had been redecorated with a spongy washdown wallpaper, ripe for sinking nails into. And it wasn't just his own initials, he added the names of his favourite bands too, the letters scratched out and replaced as his tastes changed. Fickle boy.

Vicky still couldn't quite make her mind up, but she had a little time still to get it all sorted. Rex had in fact stopped and turned round to look back, finally having noticed he had lost her. And rather than walking back to see what the problem was, he sat himself down and kept his eyes fixed straight at Vicky, knowing that the pressure of staring from ahead might make her jump to her feet and catch up quickly.

★　　★　　★

The nurses had started handling the visitors differently, knowing they knew almost as much as they did. No need to explain the tests and hourly checks any more. It gets easier in some ways when the guests stay on for more than a couple of nights. They could even offer to throw in breakfast for free to get them to stay a little longer.

The waiting room had moved whilst they re-decorated. The new one, like a dental surgery, had old magazines in the centre on a low table. The most recent was a copy of the *TV Times* from September with the crossword done. Vicky's eldest thought it would be a good idea to make sure some of their small budget was kept aside for more. It would have been inappropriate to bring your own and wait, even a paper, looking forward to reading the feature on the rise of London's members' bars where they served elaborate and expensive cocktails to models and media men. So they took turns with whatever they could find, staring at a blank TV screen when their hands were empty, too embarrassed to find a socket, plug it in and tune in for the evening's entertainment.

Sat opposite on the eighth day was a man in a leather biker's jacket. He was heavy and broad with a head as bald as his daughter's, who, after a particularly long night out clubbing, had ended up with her head cleaved open on the metal reinforcements of an A-road bridge support just south of Welwyn. He hadn't changed since then, but the leather had a stronger smell to it as the body beneath warmed it through to just the right temperature. He prayed with a bible – and one that obviously hadn't been taken out just for this special occasion – and went to call his wife on the hour whether or not he had news to give. The jacket didn't go with the book, though the colour of the leather did match. And in the same way everyone in the room seemed all of a sudden religious: girls with short skirts setting off to light candles in the chapel, scruffy middle-aged men holding tenaciously onto Mass cards with a picture of white clay praying hands on the front. A good few ministers joined and left too, but no priests in robes, just old, short, black men with white hair, leading prayers for the room in circles – everyone told to hold hands, feeling ridiculous, but not wanting to offend or upset anyone in power.

They assumed Vicky's family wouldn't know the words. So they made more noise to show them they did, and had their hands gripped even tighter as the others realised they would be some use to the circle after all.

After the eighth day Vicky's husband piled up the cards he had been sorting the weekend before, leaving one large pile in more of a mess than when he started, the day she had been brought in. No one had been in the room for a week and the curtains were still closed. How sad, they all thought, and then realised that they hadn't been open in years, Vicky having liked the pale pink light filling the room with the sun passing through the thin, cerise-coloured calico. With her out of the house, her eldest went through some of her boxes and files, finding letters she had kept from her parents and some of his baby teeth, rattling like a single maraca in the thick card case of a cocktail cigarette packet. He remembered when she had smoked those – she had only ever had two packets, given to her by her friend Joan at work. Vicky hated people going through her things but he didn't think she'd mind, it wasn't as if she had anything to hide.

In his mind he drew up a list of things he should tell a good friend to dispose of, just in case anything happened to him – old diaries definitely, but he didn't know where he had left them; things that would make people uncomfortable to sort through; things a charity shop wouldn't even want. And what about old hair brushes and clothes just off your back, still with flakes from your scalp, dead hair and the smell of working the whole day? Stuff like that surely shouldn't be left lying around to tidy up and put away. Wash even. And running his hand across his mother's old jumpers he realised that she had, in fact, always smelt of lilac soap.

Vicky had finally made her mind up. More out of laziness and a quick guess which way would be shorter. Really tired now. But she had just stood up, with one leg in each direction – like an American tourist in Greenwich – not showing her decision to Rex or the reader.

On the walls of Vicky's bedroom were a collection of postcards she'd had framed from all her favourite places: the Crowned Virgin with a six-decade rosary and yellow roses on her feet, the Black Madonna she had spotted in Croatia and another of a statue, white this time, from the pedestal opposite. All of them were covered in dust, the white plastic frames with gold paint to make them look fancy from a distance ('fancy': the word the stallholder had used to make up his sign at Wembley Market, three for a pound) all begging for a sponge down so they could look like new again. Vicky's eldest moved some of the dust away from the pictures with a finger, pushing it to the corners and making the whole thing look even dirtier, like those filthy vans, with 'clean me' etched on the bonnet as a joke by an unfunny driver, up early to start the job and not even seeing how grimy the metalwork had got. Never the best sign for the self-employed, like going for an interview without ironing your shirt.

The carpets in her bedroom were a little better, but above the headboard were two slightly discoloured circles where heads should have been. It had been a bad idea to use matt pastel yellow wallpaper just there, when it would have to help take the strain of weary necks as hours of TV were watched and books read, with eyes closing, and then out for the count until the morning, still upright and very uncomfortable. So much so that work would be a problem.

He sat down on the bed and leant over to rummage around in the low bedside cabinet. The new mattress protector slipped as he moved forward and down to get to the back of the cupboard by the bedside, the old mattress beneath with the worn edges exposed completely now to reveal the sharp sides of the spring-case. Hidden usually, but he now had to be careful not to slip off completely and end up on the floor. His mother had done that on a couple of occasions, forcing her to call for help and wait, if her children were playing their music too loudly or her husband had nipped out to buy cigarettes.

Inside was the usual fare, for her at least: a book by Sr. Bridget McKenna (no relation to the TV hypnotist) on the power of miracles, a collection of prayer cards, rosaries and medals and a few bundles of letters and invitations. He took those out, having read the book one year whilst stuck in a convent in France with his mother and aunt, and having seen enough rosaries to know what they did. The invitations were mostly for weddings – cousins in Sri Lanka and Dubai and a few names he hadn't heard of before. Probably just other relations, he presumed, just a little more distant. It was a large, sprawling family. The letters were a jumble, some from just a few months ago and others from the late '60s before they had moved to the house, along with a note for her husband to feed the cat and one to her eldest to let him know Mike would be coming to stay the week before term started again. He remembered seeing that one on the table when it was first written and wondered why she had kept it. The two telephone numbers on the reverse made it clear enough, both of them better at finding scraps of paper than going through a file or well-ordered book for important details.

There were ones from his grandfather, starting the month he had left his house in Colombo to five of his girls, to come and stay in London with the two who had left before him. Vicky was one of the five, her son looked up to the right-hand corner and saw the Colombo address. He had lost his job and the house needed work – much more the sort of job for one of his younger sons-in-law – whilst he got to see the two who got away, make sure they were working hard and extending the family further. He wasn't looking forward to a new job at sixty though, knowing already he'd not have the time and energy to work towards a car and driver to guarantee he got there in time each morning. And who would make his breakfast and get his suit ready? It was a warning to Vicky to stay and do her best, maybe find a husband there and settle down. He had seen the other side and it wasn't as idyllic as it was meant to have been. Ideas got from films and books and other false representations were tempting but not to be trusted, he told her.

He had got a new job, at a furniture shop on Tottenham Court Road, spending his days making sure families in Regent's Park got their new table and chairs in time for a dinner party, and his evenings writing letters, addressed to his daughter, hauled up in his big, old house, which he was missing desperately. Together the letters were like diary entries Vicky would bring over with her for him to file in order, having not taken his advice, to keep it all clear for when his mind started failing. One entry was about the time he had been called names as he walked along Euston Road, with the buses full, to catch the Bakerloo line to Kingsbury, the voices getting louder as he walked because the young men said he probably found their accents hard to understand, if he did in fact speak their language at all. That was what they had said to him in his old musty office in Colombo, retired early and replaced by someone who knew the old language, someone who had shown his support for the new government. So he was done with all this talking, he told Vicky, and instead had got himself involved in local church services, where he knew things like that shouldn't matter. Imagine how many languages He would be fluent in.

Vicky had obviously taken that to heart. The next

letter was addressed to her in Westbourne Park, already over, to see him safe and do the talking for him if he felt the need to be silent.

The letters were all written in indigo ink, obviously once a little brighter and more purple. The strokes went upwards to start precisely formed letters and sweeping words that flowed into long, structured sentences, controlled beautifully with proper punctuation: colons and semicolons doing the grand job of holding back the excesses, but getting the point across. So much so he had another one of his girls, his favourite, Victoria, by his side soon enough, to help him choose his suits and polish his shoes after dinner on Sunday night. Each letter was signed off the same way – yours with affection – without the need to state love itself, just that and the blessing of a kiss. The same way he would have signed a love letter, or others to his parents whilst away at university, letting them know about the day-to-day things that they'd complain about if they weren't kept informed. But mothers are good at reading between the lines. And Vicky's eldest remembered the only Woolf novel he had read twice, with Jacob's mother writing trivial things that really begged for her son to come home.

Letters could be kept and tied with red ribbons, hidden in drawers in a writing desk if they are from a lover, or at the bottom of a wardrobe in boxes, to be re-read years later. Of course Vicky's weren't quite the full set and she had used a rubber band to keep them together, one that had got brittle over the years and lost its one use, breaking when her son tried to put them back as he had found them. She wouldn't have been happy to know he had gone through her things if she had made the decision to come back.

Under the bed were more in two small suitcases, photographs as well this time, with names and a date on the back to make them easier to identify. He realised the impossibility of it all now, seeing the boxes of orange Kodak packets by the dressing table on the floor, awaiting some kind of organisation. There couldn't have been more that fifty prints carefully labelled, spanning that many years, not one for each, clusters instead recording a new addition to the family (weddings and the odd baby, those especially unrecognisable) and sometimes groups of proud owners outside newly painted houses too. One with his aunt and uncle looking less than proud, the house in the black-and-white print not the same shade as the man's crisp shirt. And Vicky's eldest remembered being told the story of how the old house had come to be that colour for twenty years when someone mixed in some burgundy by accident – meant to stain the exposed wood beams in the ceiling to match the floors – and the money had run out to buy more fresh white. It would have looked great in Notting Hill, or even just south of Shepherd's Bush where the agents had christened another London village, but the neighbours kept laughing until the whole thing was pulled down anyway, just ten years after its old master had left to live with one of his daughters and work in a shop in London. Or so the story went, they said.

Vicky's eldest couldn't help but pay as much attention to the two cases themselves – one made from thick tan-coloured card, stiffened at the corners and closed with two metal catches, and the other in a blue and green weave with a thick, stiff zip instead. Someone had actually used them once, a long time before the family holidays had started, and more than likely they had held more precious items – items for a permanent journey, before those contents were replaced with bits of paper that people stopped looking at and forgot were even there.

Vicky's eldest was on another train before he could remember what exactly had happened after he had found those photos. A jump, but a small one, in fact only two weeks and the sun was still out. The windows were much cleaner than the ones he was used to, and the reflection a lot clearer. So clear he could see the scar on his cheek, where he had nicked himself with his razor the previous morning. Still an angry mark. The fields were flat and green and there was even a woman in a blue uniform to sell him a beer. Pity she couldn't prevent the odd looks he got buying one, when the other passengers opted for an orange juice. It was 12 already, so he took a gulp and looked out of the window and thought a little about what had happened.

The idea of sitting still for any longer was almost painful. Not in a physical sense of course, but in the way that a head plays tricks on a body that's not tired enough to fall asleep at the end of the day, after a long, hard session sitting on a swivelling chair behind a desk. Vicky's family needed a good run, to work their limbs and lungs like their heads had been over the time that had passed so far. Fortunately for Vicky's husband the journeys back and forth were enough to make him sleep quite soundly each night, but Vicky's children could never manage to shut their eyes when they knew they should try to, her daughter in particular who was wishing she had told their mother that she was expecting another child, a grandson worth keeping her eyes open for. Each usually had different sleeping habits anyway: Vicky's daughter up early, woken by her own daughter ready to get the day started with the sun bright, Vicky's younger son a little later to catch the bus to the plant at Calshott, and her eldest later still, with no real need for an alarm clock unless he had a few days in an office and a time sheet to fill. All this was much closer to Vicky's eldest's routine, making her younger boy, after a week in his old room and the chance for half an hour extra each morning to lie in, feel strange, like he wasn't making the effort. Thankfully Vicky's daughter had her own family to take care of, keep her occupied before she left for her daily visit.

Vicky had decided to take another look back, and thankfully this time most of them were there to see it. A half-raised eye was all they were getting for now. Maybe later she'd shock them all, pop both of them open and ask for something proper to eat. They could all see it happening, it was what she was like. She looked better after the rest in fact. Her belly had subsided, looking more like a five-month-old foetus than a fully grown baby impatient to come out, and her skin – she always did have good skin – was plump and smooth even around her closed mouth and eyes. Roots were starting to show in her hair and if she thought no one was going to think it strange her daughter would have brought in something to touch up her last job. For now anyway, until she was well enough to have her head over a sink with the half-washed-out dye dripping back down her neck to the rim of a pink nightie from Debenhams. A new one of course. People would come over and bring them for her, like it was a uniform she had to wear as she rested to get better. And the more she had, the easier it would be to convalesce. She still had a selection in the linen chest at the foot of her bed from 1987, when she had had her appendix out. She didn't like to take them out of their plastic bags and get them dirty when one of her son's baggy old T-shirts would do perfectly well.

That son, her elder boy, the one who owned all the big T-shirts, sat in the waiting room while his father, younger brother and sister had their lunch and ate all Vicky's grapes. Food brought as a present for her but kept out of the room in case they spread anything nasty, left instead to keep the visitors occupied and nourished. It amazed him how many bunches had gathered on the side table by the sink – making the clinical basin, fitted with those taps you can turn on and off with an elbow like a surgeon in preparation, look more homely – considering the patients them-selves were all in comas. The ward resembled a scene from a sci-fi series, when the pretty blonde (wearing glasses to make her clever-looking) and her lumbering partner in skintight denim find a chamber full of people held in stasis. To be eaten by aliens or sent through space to other planets.

Vicky's eldest liked it by himself, having the freedom to come and go and walk through corridors and up and down stairs. No one about to make him feel uncomfortable, with the space for some silence until he decided he wanted to speak. In fact he could do this for ages. Looking pensive, and quite poised, sitting on a bench in the square with people passing by and looking and wondering what was going through his head. Very calm, with the opportunity to look up at the sky and think what shade it was today with thoughtful precision. He didn't get the time to do that very often, or rather did but always felt like there were better things to be doing, even with no work on for the week. Things like reading the papers to find out what's going on, writing letters and making sure your finances are in order. Even the most relaxed housewife can fill up her days and find a need to get up early with a sense of duty, urgency even. To make the weekend count, he supposed. There was nothing else like the Friday feeling, he had heard.

Chapter Nine

Vicky had come full circle, and then back again. Up on her feet and walking quickly now to join Rex and get on with it, before it got dark or she changed her mind. Sometimes things just had to be done, got on with and thought about later.

As she started off so did he, much faster than she could ever get him to go before, and for once his size came into focus – his two large feet moving forward, left right left right, covering more ground than her small ones could possibly manage, even running. Within a minute he was out of sight. How stupid, she didn't have a watch, how could she know how long it took? But it didn't seem a very long while at all. And she surprised herself by not chasing after him, having done a little too much of that with the boys in the playground when she had actually been six.

It didn't matter anymore. She knew it would be clear enough where to go from here on in, now that a decision had been made and a little of the meaning had been chewed over in her head. He must have been a kind of pacemaker, she thought, annoyed that she hadn't seen that one coming. Much better an enticement to get her on her way than dangling a carrot a foot ahead. Who would chase after a carrot after all? Something with a little fat in it maybe, or syrup, to make it alluring. But things like that would have been too difficult to suspend from a thin piece of string, without it all falling apart to lay quivering, in a mess, on the floor. And who would have held the pole aloft without her seeing them doing it?

The things that went through her head. And just a few minutes before she had had grand ideas unfolding: full, old memories, and a whole lot of big decisions to make, leaving her finally with a wry, knowing smile on her small, round face.

The clouds had come out and the whole scene was made cosier for her, shortening the height above her head and making the bright blue sky less overwhelming. The road ahead was enough to contend with, stretching on still and much wider now she was on it. Even the sun got off her back and let her get on with the job of walking, veiled by a soft, white cloud like a fat, ripe cheese wrapped in cloth to keep it fresh for when it was needed.

Looking down she saw her shoes were clean. Her dress wasn't too bad either. No sign of dirt from the ground, which was good considering how long she had been sitting. Not even those deep creases you get from picnicking in the park, in a light summer dress that shouldn't really be sat down in. How Vicky managed to know that for sure was difficult to tell – her head tried to crane round as her hands smoothed the pale linen from her waist to the top of her thighs, and without an incredibly long neck she had to assume all was straight and correct. Ready for it now and looking quite smart.

The path wasn't dusty – good for keeping her clean shoes looking new – or too damp either, like the wet lawns at garden parties when heels sink in and dew dimples the browning tips of soft, cream-coloured leather. That wouldn't do at all. Vicky had no idea who she was on her way to meet but there was always a chance they might care even if she didn't, looking down and inspecting the details without listening to what she had to say.

As she walked Vicky took time to focus in on the other little things too: nails, hair, and the corner of her mouth, which she touched now with her left index finger, softly, and again, just in case she had something she shouldn't have hanging out, a token reminder of lunch. All in order, she thought, without the benefit of a mirror or the objective eye of a friend. It felt suddenly as if she were going for an interview or, better still, meeting an in-law, checking her appearance first in the car mirror and again in the glass pane of a front door, a little too late by then to do anything anyway. She hadn't had the opportunity to do that in the flesh before, but she had done it with her husband's friends; all in a circle around a table in The Black Lion waiting for one of their group to bring her in and convince them she wouldn't change the dynamic. In fact Vicky's appearance hadn't mattered as much then as it did now – their acceptance had always been just a short way off, not something they had thought seriously about retaining. Much more worrying was the two-month wait as her soon-to-be mother-in-law inspected the picture she had been sent in the post by her son. She had even gone to meet Vicky's remaining sisters still close to her home to fill out the image, to give it some depth and background with the reassurance of family resemblances. Thankfully she had approved, based on the little she had in front of her, and sent her best in a telegram that they saved to read out last at the wedding.

Vicky's children had it very different, with arguments about changing loyalties, and difficult personalities, filling her house as one of their friends found someone too quickly, moved to Bath and got a good, sound job and new wife. A good broker too, to help with mortgages and long-term investments for the future. There had been a spate of that lately. Vicky could never decide who was right, supposedly having a very different idea of it all herself. She had gone ten years before making those kinds of decisions when people really did look at her strangely, with her giving the impression she might opt out completely.

Enough of that nonsense. None of it mattered, certainly not here and not now. Vicky had no doubt they'd be enough distraction if she chose to go looking for it.

Everywhere she looked reminded her of something, some things a little more obvious than others. The tree on her left – a quick run to let her hand feel its way down the rough trunk – reminded her of one she had seen before. Perhaps the apple tree in the garden by the bench her husband had made out of two stumps and an old floor board (still able to bear weight, remarkably) or one she had sat beneath in Soho Square after a short lunchtime Adoration of the Holy Sacrament at St. Patrick's. Who knew? There were a million more to get it mistaken with, a million other moments held like pictures in her mind with backgrounds only seen fully by the one taking the picture. It was silly to worry about it now when she had always found faces and names hard enough.

Vicky kept on with the walk, stopping less and less as she went on. Now and again she would see something that deserved a closer inspection, but she had grown fussier. To think she had found a tree interesting. Now it would have to *do* something quite fantastic to impress her. In the distance she saw that the path narrowed again – she wished it would make its mind up

– and on both sides it was lined with red stone, half-buried in the ground with the other half sitting square out in the air to reach a two-foot peak; marking out the ground with the precision of Vicky's own clay lawn border tiles.

They came into focus quickly, and on each sat a person, some she knew and many others she couldn't place. All sitting and focusing on themselves, looking through her when they lifted their heads up. Resting hard and thinking like she had done a while ago now. None of them sure, even though they were so close, it made her think whether it was worth more thought. But Vicky had already decided not to do that again and walked past them all: old men looking at their feet and young girls, frightened and unsure why they were here, looking around for the comfort of an adult hand. She wondered how old they all really were; after all she wasn't six, even if she looked it. The crowd built up as she walked; without places to sit they stood on idly, milling about, avoiding eye contact and thinking still. It all looked like hard work, Vicky thought.

Luckily she was small enough and nimble, could weave through without disruption. Her eldest would have loved that skill late on Friday when people queued to get into dank basement bars, moisture dripping from ceilings, and at the end of the night on the way home, as the black cabs disappeared and Said on Wardour Street rallied his three brothers in people-carriers. But what to do when she got there, Vicky wondered. Would there be two men with a guest list and a scrutinous eye?

Pushing forward she finally found an empty space, making room for her and her decision. And beyond her a simple set of swing doors, not at all what she had expected, no golden gates or man in white waiting to usher her in. A simple push was all it would take, the hinges greased, making it easy for her weak arms. And so Vicky took the final step, her arms outstretched, finding herself in a small room with a single bed and noise trying to get in through the walls with people laughing and talking loudly in languages she'd never got round to learning, as music played and they danced.

She'd join them in the morning, have a good drink and get talking to her new neighbours. But first a long sleep, it had been a tiring journey. From the only window set high in the wall she could see the cloudy full face of the moon, filtering the light it had stolen, holding it back for a more appropriate time. What Vicky needed was darkness, so she lay down and flicked the switch, closing her eyes to clear the picture. Now it was quiet enough for her to sleep and dream. The end of this story would be all her own.

More fiction from Burning House

The Wrecking Ball
Christiana Spens

'Christiana Spens writes beautifully about the taste
for oblivion, the temptation of the abyss, the alluring
mystery of nothingness. Truth is its soul and brevity is
its body.'
Sebastian Horsley, author of *Dandy in the Underworld*

'Razor-sharp prose that's soaked with authenticity.'
Anna David, author of *Party Girl*

Published May 2008
ISBN: 9781905636198
£7.99

www.burninghousebooks.com

More fiction from Burning House

A Clockwork Apple
Belinda Webb

'Dark, highly lyrical...this brave, pithy debut kicks you in the face, while making a mockery of bureaucratic society.'
Dazed and Confused

'A remarkably confident piece of writing...Webb delights in playing linguistic games and riffs continually on Burgess's teenspeak.'
New Statesman

Published April 2008
ISBN: 9781905636174
£7.99

www.burninghousebooks.com